HOMETOWN HEARTS

SHIPMENT 1

Stranger in Town by Brenda Novak
Baby's First Homecoming by Cathy McDavid
Her Surprise Hero by Abby Gaines
A Mother's Homecoming by Tanya Michaels
A Firefighter in the Family by Trish Milburn
Tempted by a Texan by Mindy Neff

SHIPMENT 2

It Takes a Family by Victoria Pade
The Sheriff of Heartbreak County by Kathleen Creighton
A Hometown Boy by Janice Kay Johnson
The Renegade Cowboy Returns by Tina Leonard
Unexpected Bride by Lisa Childs
Accidental Hero by Loralee Lillibridge

SHIPMENT 3

An Unlikely Mommy by Tanya Michaels
Single Dad Sheriff by Lisa Childs
In Protective Custody by Beth Cornelison
Cowboy to the Rescue by Trish Milburn
The Ranch She Left Behind by Kathleen O'Brien
Most Wanted Woman by Maggie Price
A Weaver Wedding by Allison Leigh

SHIPMENT 4

A Better Man by Emilie Rose
Daddy Protector by Jacqueline Diamond
The Road to Bayou Bridge by Liz Talley
Fully Engaged by Catherine Mann
The Cowboy's Secret Son by Trish Milburn
A Husband's Watch by Karen Templeton

HOMETOWN HEARTS

Her Sister's Secret Life

USA TODAY Bestselling Author

PAMELA TOTH

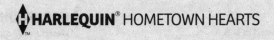

HARLEQUIN® HOMETOWN HEARTS

Recycling programs
for this product may
not exist in your area.

ISBN-13: 978-0-373-21478-5

Her Sister's Secret Life

Copyright © 2007 by Pamela Toth

All rights reserved. Except for use in any review, the reproduction or utilization of this work in whole or in part in any form by any electronic, mechanical or other means, now known or hereinafter invented, including xerography, photocopying and recording, or in any information storage or retrieval system, is forbidden without the written permission of the publisher, Harlequin Enterprises Limited, 225 Duncan Mill Road, Don Mills, Ontario M3B 3K9, Canada.

This is a work of fiction. Names, characters, places and incidents are either the product of the author's imagination or are used fictitiously, and any resemblance to actual persons, living or dead, business establishments, events or locales is entirely coincidental.

This edition published by arrangement with Harlequin Books S.A.

For questions and comments about the quality of this book, please contact us at CustomerService@Harlequin.com.

® and TM are trademarks of Harlequin Enterprises Limited or its corporate affiliates. Trademarks indicated with ® are registered in the United States Patent and Trademark Office, the Canadian Intellectual Property Office and in other countries.

HARLEQUIN®
www.Harlequin.com

Printed in U.S.A.

When she was growing up in Seattle, *USA TODAY* bestselling author **Pamela Toth** planned to be an artist, not a writer. It was only after her mother, a librarian, gave her a stack of Harlequin romances that Pam began to dream about a writing career. However, her plans were postponed while she raised two daughters and worked full-time. Then fate stepped in. Through a close friend, Pam found a fledgling local chapter of Romance Writers of America, and for the next twenty years she belonged to a close-knit group of published writers while penning romances for several lines at Harlequin. When Pam isn't traveling with her husband, she loves spending time with her two grown daughters, antiquing, gardening, cross-stitching and reading.

To everyone who waits for a loved one to return home safely, from a date, from a trip or from a war. To my husband, Frank. Priceless.

Chapter One

Steve Lindstrom liked getting to the job site before the rest of his crew. This first, solitary half hour gave him a chance to look around without someone bugging him with a question about building specs or material deliveries. He could savor the progress of something born of his vision, his investment and—in large part—by his own sweat.

He stood by his truck, sipping his coffee as he watched the streaky pink-and-gold sunrise fade quickly above the jagged ridge of the Cascade Mountains far to the east. Construction was always a gamble, but a hot market and his own growing reputation had enabled him to buy this piece of choice view property. On it rose a sprawling wooden skeleton that was slowly becoming his fanciest house yet, as well as his largest financial gamble to date. Nearby stood another house, nearly as grand and almost completed.

Since Steve had first begun working as a framer during summer vacations, the work had always given him a sense of accomplishment that was nearly as sweet as throwing a football into his receiver's waiting hands or acing a tough exam. Now he was the boss. The control, the decisions and the headaches connected with Lindstrom Construction were his responsibility.

From Admiralty Inlet, where sailboats dotted the choppy water, came a light breeze scented with salt and sunshine. Above a nearby stand of arrow-straight Douglas fir trees, an eagle soared. Its white head was easy to identify against the blue sky, its wingspan a sight to behold. For the moment, a sense of peace settled on the clearing with its ribbon of road and two new buildings.

Setting aside his empty mug, Steve grabbed a clipboard and scowled at his notes on material shipments and subcontractors' schedules. Juggling two projects was taking its toll.

One late delivery, one installation problem, and his time frame would collapse like a row of dominoes.

Since he'd heard that Lily Mayfield was back in town, his concentration had been shot to hell when he needed it the most. The possibility of running into her nagged him like the dull throb of a bad tooth. Over the years, his memories of Lily had begun to fade, but the possibility of turning a corner and running into her again, of drowning in her sky-blue eyes and getting drunk on her scent, made him think of little else.

He kicked aside a fist-sized rock so that no one would trip on it, wishing he had an excuse to swing a sledgehammer and demolish something instead of making nice with his designer and soothing his nervous banker's nerves.

As Steve checked out the three-car garage that had been framed in yesterday, the sound of a truck engine cut into his concentration. He looked up to see his friend Wade Garrett's pickup coming down the long dirt driveway. Slowly, it bounced over the ruts to avoid raising dust. Wade had been bunking at Steve's house, but he hadn't found his way home last night.

Steve watched Wade park his rig and walk up the driveway. He was as tall as Steve, but leaner in his T-shirt and faded jeans. A base-ball cap covered his cropped black hair. The grin on his angular face was that of a man who had recently rolled out of someone else's bed after a night of memorable sex.

Steve felt a twinge of envy. When was the last time he'd had terrific sex—or any sex at all? He could barely remember.

"I didn't expect you to be here today," Steve said as Wade joined him.

Wade worked for him part-time, but lately he'd been talking about returning to his former profession of investment broker.

"I'm not working today, old buddy. I'm celebrating." Wade slapped Steve's back enthusiastically. "If it wasn't so damned early, I'd buy you a beer."

Steve eyed his scruffy-jawed friend warily. "You just win the lottery or get laid by a high-priced hooker?" he drawled.

In the few months he'd known Wade, Steve couldn't remember ever seeing him so fired up. In fact, he'd been moping around since a recent breakup with his girlfriend, Pauline Mayfield, who just happened to be Lily's older sister.

"Hey, pal, what I'm high on is better than

money," Wade replied with a laugh. "Way better."

"You've hooked up with someone," Steve guessed, propping his shoulder against a corner post. "Who's the lucky lady?"

Wade shook his head. "It's not what you think, but I did want you to be the first to hear my news."

"The guys will be here any minute now and you look ready to bust a gut, so you'd better spill," Steve replied. "What's up with you?"

Wade's cheeks were flushed and he practically twitched with excitement. "Pauline and I are back together." With a wild whoop that startled a crow off a nearby branch, he tossed his cap high into the air. "We're getting married."

"Congratulations, man!" Steve exclaimed, happy for them both. He grasped Wade's outstretched hand and pulled him into a bear hug, slapping his back before releasing him.

No wonder Wade was acting like a crazy man. He had been nuts about Pauline since he first rented the apartment above her converted carriage house.

It would have been selfish of Steve to wish Wade could have fallen for someone else, just because of Steve and Lily's history. Just because she was back in town with a twelve-year-old son he knew nothing about, a boy who everyone said looked just like Steve.

"My God," he exclaimed after he'd let go of Wade, "no wonder you're grinning like a damned idiot. You're marrying up in the world, that's for sure."

"True enough," Wade agreed as the throaty whine of a motorcycle signaled the imminent arrival of Steve's crew.

"Time for me to get to work," he told Wade, "but I'll buy the first round at the Crab Pot tonight. Bring Pauline so I can tell her what a poor choice she's made."

"I'll see what she says," Wade replied, sounding married already.

Carlos roared up on his Harley, followed by George in his faded red pickup.

"I've got a favor to ask," Wade told Steve as the men began unloading their gear. "Would you stand up with me at the wedding? It'll be toward the end of September and we're keeping it small."

Wade cleared his throat. "I know it's a lot to ask—" he added. So he'd noticed Steve's reaction to Lily's voice on the answering machine when she had left a message for Wade. Steve had been caught off guard, that was all, but Wade had obviously drawn his own conclusion.

Here's the opportunity to prove she's just a bad memory, whispered a voice in Steve's head. Now that Pauline and Lily had patched up their differences, his ex-girlfriend would no doubt be part of her sister's wedding and her life, but he wasn't about to let Lily's presence scare him away.

"Don't talk stupid," Steve said gruffly, ignoring the sudden tightness in his gut. "I'm honored that you asked me, okay?"

Wade's frown cleared. "Thanks, man."

"Hey, Frisco, you working today?" Carlos shouted, using the nickname he'd given Wade. "That means I can goof off, right, boss?"

"Wrong," Steve replied, slapping Wade's back. "He's got better things to do than pound nails." He turned back to his friend. "Nice work. You've landed yourself a fantastic woman."

The rest of it, Steve wouldn't let it be a problem. He would deal. Lily was part of his past and that's where she was going to stay.

Lily Mayfield and her sister stood on the sidewalk in front of Pauline's cross-stitch shop, Uncommon Threads. It took up part of the ground floor of an old building in the historic business district in Crescent Cove.

"I still can't get over how much everything grew while I was gone." Lily looked down the busy street at the flower baskets and banners hanging from the ornate antique light poles. Half of the storefronts had been empty thirteen years ago.

"You've been home long enough to adjust to the changes," Pauline replied as she studied the display in her front window. "Did you think everything was going to stay frozen in time until you decided to come back?"

"No, of course not." Lily glanced at her watch. It was nearly time to pick up her son, Jordan, from his friend's house.

"What do you think?" Pauline frowned at the window display. "Too busy? Too cutesy?"

Lily considered the plain clay pots that were arranged in front of a white picket fence. A round hoop framing an embroidered flower picture was stuck into each pot like a lollypop.

"It's clever," she decided. "If I wasn't all thumbs, I'd be tempted to buy a kit myself."

Pauline didn't appear convinced as she fiddled with a strand of streaky blond hair that was several shades darker than Lily's.

"I hope you're right," she murmured. "With all the tour buses coming from Seattle and down from Canada, I'm really hoping to attract some new customers."

"I've got to get Jordan," Lily told her. "Don't forget to make some time in your schedule to plan your wedding. September will be here before we know it." On this bright July day, fall was hard to imagine.

Pauline gave a helpless shrug. "I thought a small backyard ceremony would be simple. If it rains, we'll move it inside."

Lily wanted to roll her eyes at her sister's naiveté. The living room of the old Victorian was huge, but the furnishings were getting shabby.

"Simple and yet elegant," Lily said with a grin. "Don't worry. I'll help you." Planning Pauline's wedding together was something Lily wouldn't have dreamed possible two months ago, but now she was looking forward to it.

"Congratulations again, Paulie." She gave her sister a hug. "Wade's a lucky man."

Pauline shook her head. "I'm the lucky one. Thanks for the ride. He's picking me up, so I'll see you at home."

With a flip of her hand, Lily hurried around

her car, which was parked at the curb, and slid behind the wheel. In her opinion, they were *both* lucky. Wade was a great guy, but Pauline was a wonderful sister.

Lily thanked the stars that she was also a forgiving one. Taking advantage of a break in the line of slow-moving traffic, Lily pulled out. She glanced back in time to see that Pauline was still standing on the sidewalk. She waved at someone coming up the street.

As the big white pickup drew parallel to Lily's car, she looked up curiously. The driver's face was partially hidden by sunglasses and a baseball cap topped his shaggy, sun-bleached hair, but his smile was instantly recognizable.

Even after all this time.

For an instant, his gaze seemed to meet hers despite his dark lenses. Her hands choked the wheel and she looked away, right at the black lettering on the door of his truck.

Lindstrom Construction.

She jerked her gaze back upward for another look, but she was too late. He had driven on by as though nothing earthshaking had just occurred.

Lily had known that she couldn't live in Crescent Cove for long without running into Steve. Despite the new growth and the tourists, this was still basically the same small town where they had grown up together. She'd thought she was prepared for the first sight of him, the boy who'd captured her heart, but she'd been fooling herself. Shame and regret for the way she had treated him still rose up to choke her whenever she thought about facing him again.

And face him she would need to do someday soon. She owed him that much, but she just wasn't ready.

Had he recognized her? She was probably nothing more to him now than an unpleasant memory. The idea made her sad as she stared at his departing truck in her rearview mirror.

"Lily, watch out!" Pauline cried out in warning.

Lily jerked her attention back to where it belonged just in time to see that the car in front of her had stopped to parallel park. Lily jammed on her brakes, barely avoiding a collision.

"Damn it," she exclaimed, hoping Steve hadn't glanced back and noticed what she had nearly done.

"Are you okay?" Pauline gazed at Lily through the open passenger window. "Did you see…?"

"I'm fine!" Lily snapped, irritation and embarrassment sharpening her tone. It wasn't her sister's fault that she had acted like an idiot.

The driver in front of her changed his mind about the parking spot, giving her an escape. With a sheepish smile and a quick wave, Lily drove away with a sigh of relief. If she was lucky, Pauline would have forgotten about the incident by the time she got home.

Too bad Lily couldn't do the same. Feeling like the same coward she had been at eighteen, she went to pick up the boy who made everything she had gone through worthwhile—and the reason she owed Steve an explanation.

Good God Almighty! When Steve had noticed the attractive blonde and seen her shocked expression, the jolt of recognition nearly spun his head around. Two blocks down Harbor Avenue he turned abruptly into a parking lot, scaring two pedestrians who were about to step in front of his truck. Before he could hit the log barrier that prevented vehicles from driving into the bay, he braked hard and killed the engine.

A brief glimpse hadn't been enough to indicate how much thirteen years had changed

Lily. Had time tarnished her beauty, stamping her face with the same coldness that had chilled her uncaring heart? Furious with himself for giving two hoots, he slapped the steering wheel with the flat of his hand and swore again, earning himself a startled glance from an approaching fisherman. The man veered away as he walked by Steve, making him feel even more stupid.

He glanced at the cell phone next to him on the seat, tempted to call Wade, but he wasn't going to let one little Lily sighting turn him into a hysterical wimp. He'd do the manly thing, suck it up and go straight to the Crab Pot, a local tavern. After he'd downed a few brewskies to take off the edge, he would ask Wade to drive him home.

The only hitch in his plan was that it was too damned early to execute it. When he'd spotted Lily, he'd been on his way to the builders' supply store. Resigned to postponing his meltdown, he fired up the truck and swung around so he could pull back out onto the street. As he did so, a redhead in a yellow convertible honked and waved. Her smile was a welcome reminder that the world was full of friendly women. There was no point in wasting time—or beer—over one old fish who had gotten away.

Just as he reached his destination with his equilibrium restored, he got a call from Carlos at the job site.

Now what? Steve thought as he answered his cell. "Yeah," he replied brusquely.

"Hey, boss, can you bring us some burgers from the Shack?" Carlos asked. "We're starving out here."

Steve climbed out of his truck, phone at his ear. "Depends," he drawled, nodding at a guy coming out the front door. "You got the kitchen framed in yet?"

Lily drove slowly through the old part of town on the bluff above the waterfront, listening to her son's chatter as she headed to the family home on Cedar Street where they had been staying with Pauline.

"Cory's got an Xbox," Jordan exclaimed. He'd hardly taken a breath since Lily had picked him up at the house of one of his new friends. "We played his new skateboarding game."

Their move to Crescent Cove had been dicey at first because he'd been homesick for LA and he was still grieving for their long-time friend and Lily's guardian angel, Francis Yost. After growing up on Francis's spacious estate, Jordan had made it clear to Lily that he wanted nothing to do with Crescent Cove.

Lucky for her, Pauline's fiancé had stepped in to help, spending time with Jordan until he met a few boys his own age. Wade's friendship with Lily had initially given Pauline the wrong impression when she'd walked in on him with Lily in his arms, comforting her after an argument with her son. Fortunately that had been resolved and they had all moved on.

"So you had a good time?" she asked Jordan now. "You remembered to thank Cory's mother for putting up with you?"

He lifted his ball cap to run one hand through his thick blond hair. It needed a trim, she noted silently.

"Aw, Mom," he drawled on a long-suffering sigh, "I always remember that stuff. You've drilled it into me since I was born." He repositioned the cap and tugged down the bill. "I bet you even used to tell me when I was growing in your belly."

She turned onto Cedar, a narrow, tree-lined street of historical Victorian homes in various stages of disrepair. "It's my mission in life to tame you and turn you into a cultured individual," she teased.

Instead of making a comeback, he turned

to look at her intently. "Is it true that my real dad lives around here?" he asked. "And that I look just like him?"

The question shouldn't have come as so much of a surprise. Did she think kids didn't overhear things?

"Where did you hear that?" she asked, shamelessly stalling for time as she turned into their driveway and drove past the house that had been named Mayfield Manor by one of her ancestors. Braking in front of the detached garage, she was startled to see that her hand was shaking when she reached for the gearshift.

She glanced at Jordan to see if he had noticed.

"Ryan MacPherson was teasing me when he came over to Cory's, but then Cory's mom sent him home."

"Good for Michelle," Lily replied fervently. Back in the day, Lily had been chosen over Ryan's mother for the lead in a high school play. The former Heather Rolfe had probably never forgiven Lily. It sounded as though Heather was still a witch.

Lily's first impulse was to go over and confront the other mother for gossiping in front of Ryan, but she couldn't very well blame

Heather for saying aloud what half the town was at least thinking.

"Is it true?" Jordan persisted. "Does my dad live here in this stupid town?"

Lily was saved from answering by the sight of Wade approaching her car.

"We'll have to talk later," she told Jordan as Wade leaned down and grinned at them through the open passenger window.

"Okay with you if I kidnap your kid for a couple of hours?" he asked Lily. "Hey, sport! Want to go shoot some hoops?"

Lord, yes, she thought gratefully. "He's got to eat first," she replied.

"I ate at Cory's." Jordan got out of the car and returned Wade's high five. "Can I go? Please, Mom?"

Obviously he didn't mind postponing the subject of his paternity. Silently, Lily vowed to deal with it soon, just as soon as she figured out how much to tell him before she went and talked to Steve.

What a mess.

She emerged behind the wheel, realizing that both males were still waiting for her to say something. "Sure, you can go. Take some water with you and don't forget to actually drink it."

Wade rested a paternal hand on Jordan's

bony shoulder, winking at her over the boy's head. "I'll take good care of him, ma'am."

"I know you will," she replied, returning his smile. "Thanks."

"I gotta change shoes," Jordan said. "Be right back."

"Is everything okay?" Wade asked Lily as soon as her son was out of earshot. "Did I interrupt something?"

Next to her sister, Wade was probably the last person Lily dared confide in. Regretfully, she shook her head. "Nothing that won't wait, and it's good for him to spend time with you."

"Makes a nice break for me, too," Wade replied as he followed her through the gate in the picket fence enclosing Pauline's backyard.

"A respite from wedding plans?" Lily teased over her shoulder. Even a perfect male— Pauline's assessment of her fiancé—would have a breaking point when it came to deciding the myriad details necessary for even a simple wedding: guests, invitations, clothing, music, food. The list went on.

He flashed his heart-stopping grin. "Please, please don't tell Pauline. She's already having so much fun with this."

"I won't breathe a word," Lily promised, crossing her heart solemnly before she went up the back steps. Before she could open the screen door that Jordan had let slam behind him, Wade reached up and touched her arm.

"Lily, wait a second."

She figured that he must need help with something to do with the nuptials, but his expression was one of concern.

"I wanted you to know that I've asked Steve to be my best man," he said quietly. "Given the history between you two, I hope it's not going to be a problem for you, but he's become a good friend since I came here."

Everyone knew that Steve had been her steady boyfriend for two years before she had suddenly left town. Wade was aware that she hadn't told Steve her plans or spoken to him since.

Deliberately, she plastered on a wide smile. "I'm fine with it," she exclaimed, seeing his shoulders slump in relief. "He and I are ancient history."

She was surprised when Wade's frown didn't lessen. "Have you talked to him yet?" he probed.

She lifted her brows, feigning ignorance. "About what?"

Wade's glance flicked toward the house

and then back to her face. "I know it's none of my business—" he began.

"But I appreciate your concern," Lily cut in as she opened the screen door. She didn't want Jordan to overhear them. "I'm parched," she continued. "Want some lemonade?"

Wade reached for a sports bag hanging on a hook in the laundry room. "No, thanks, but if you want to talk…" His voice trailed off when Jordan pounded down the staircase.

The knot in Lily's stomach tightened when he appeared in the kitchen seconds later wearing his old Lakers tank top and baggy shorts. More than anything, she wanted to protect him from ever being hurt or disappointed, even though she knew it was an unrealistic goal.

"Hey, buddy, grab me one, too," Wade said as Jordan opened the door to the refrigerator and removed a bottled water.

Tucking his basketball under his arm, he complied. "See ya, Mom," he said as he walked past Lily.

She was stunned to realize how much he'd shot up in the past few months. Before she knew it, he would be all grown-up. Without a shred of remorse, she refused to think of the years his father had already missed.

Before Wade followed Jordan out the door,

he gave her a hard look. "The boy deserves the truth."

"You don't know what you're asking," Lily whispered after Wade had closed the door behind him.

Could Jordan handle the truth? Could any of them?

Chapter Two

"I thought we were going to the park," Jordan said, frowning out the window of Wade's truck as they went down an unfamiliar street.

Would Jordan ever learn his way around this stupid burg? Back in LA, he knew which buses to take to all the important places when his mom didn't have time to drive him: the skateboard park, the closest mall, the library and a couple of his buddies' houses. Crescent Cove didn't even *have* buses except for the Greyhound that stopped out on the highway once a day. When he'd asked his mom if he could ride the ferry to Seattle by himself, she'd practically freaked.

The street they were on was narrow and curvy with patches all over the pavement. Tree branches dipped low, making Jordan feel as though they were going down a green tunnel.

"I have to run an errand first," Wade replied. "A friend of mine forgot some papers he needs, so we're going to drop them off at his building site."

Wade stared straight ahead, looking like he wasn't happy about it.

"Are you and your friend in a fight?" Jordan asked. "You look mad."

He didn't like it when people argued. Francis, his and Mom's friend back in California, always spoke softly except when he got mad at his partner, Augustine, for charging too many clothes on his credit card. Then Jordan could hear their angry voices clear over in the guest house where he and his mom lived.

Had lived until Francis dropped dead right in his fancy kitchen. After that, Mom said she guessed it was time to come home, he reminded himself. Except this totally lame and boring town would never feel like home to Jordan. It didn't have a skateboard park or a cinema, except for one tiny old theater that showed art films, whatever they were.

His question must have surprised Wade,

because when he finally turned his head, his dark brows had climbed up his forehead, making wrinkles.

"No, I'm not fighting with him," Wade replied. "Why would you think that? He's my buddy, same as you."

Jordan shrugged, feeling self-conscious. He would never understand grown-ups, not even when he became one himself. "Wow. He's building a house?" he asked. "Can I see it?"

Wade grinned and Jordan was able to relax again.

"He's building two houses, but one is nearly done. We'll have to wear hard hats around the other one," Wade cautioned. "I'll even show you the framing I did."

"Cool," Jordan exclaimed eagerly, even though he wasn't sure what framing had to do with anything. Back in California, he had driven by houses that were only partly finished, of course, but not to stop and walk through them. This might be nearly as much fun as shooting hoops.

"Steve's a neat guy," Wade added in the same casual tone that adults used when they said *the shot won't hurt* or *your new school will be great*. "You'll like him."

Jordan wasn't fooled for a minute. He'd

heard about Steve from Cory's pal, Ryan, when he'd said that Steve was Jordan's real dad. Sure, Jordan was curious about him, but he wasn't sure that he was ready to actually *meet* the guy face-to-face. What if Steve acted disappointed?

Suddenly he wished he'd worn his new Sonics shirt instead of his old tank top, and that he hadn't argued when Mom said he needed a haircut.

"Maybe you could go later, after you dropped me off at Aunt Pauline's," he suggested uncertainly as he wet the tip of his finger and rubbed a chocolate stain on the leg of his shorts.

"What's the matter?" Wade asked as he slowed to make another turn. The houses were farther apart here, with pastures and stables mixed in between them. There were more fir trees, too. "A minute ago you were excited about it."

"Nothing," Jordan denied automatically. "I just remembered that Mom wants me home early today." He hated the way his voice squeaked, but he felt as though someone had hold of his neck, choking off his air.

Wade reached over and patted his knee. "It's okay," he said, his calm tone reminding Jordan of the way Francis spoke when he wanted him to try something new, like jumping off the diving board into the pool, which turned out to be pretty fun, or tasting sushi for the first time. Gross.

"Just say hi, all right? It won't be anything heavy, I promise." Wade grinned. "Besides, aren't you a little bit curious?"

Jordan looked at him sharply, but he was watching the road ahead where a truck pulling a huge boat was going really slow. It was almost as though he and Jordan were talking in a secret code, discussing one thing while they really meant something else.

Again Jordan shrugged, even though Wade wasn't watching him. "I guess." He wondered if his mom knew where they were going. Maybe she had even *asked* Wade to do it, so she wouldn't have to deal with it herself.

If Steve really was Jordan's dad, wouldn't she have said something a long time ago? Jordan had never *heard* of Steve before they moved to Crescent Cove.

He and his mom talked about all kinds of stuff, like not telling people that they didn't actually live in the big house with Francis or letting on that Augustine wasn't really the gardener. She had even told Jordan that the reason they had never visited Aunt Paulie before now was because Mom had done something that had really, really hurt her feelings. Something that made Mom cry when she talked about it. She said she had just gotten something in her eye, but he knew better. He was really curious because he couldn't imagine her ever doing anything that bad, but he'd been afraid to ask and make her cry again.

When they had first come here, Aunt Paulie hadn't acted happy to see them at all, even though she tried to pretend. She had been nice to Jordan right from the beginning, though, and he thought it would be okay. Then something happened to make her mad at his mom again. Wade moved out of the apartment over the garage and went to stay with Steve for a while, but that was way before Ryan had blabbed about him being Jordan's *biological* father.

Now Aunt Paulie was engaged to Wade and everybody was going nuts about their wedding. Wade had even teased Jordan about walking up the aisle with a basket of rose petals, as if all the powers in the universe could make him do anything *that* embarrassing.

Jordan was really, really relieved that Wade

had been joking. It was bad enough that Mom insisted that he would have to wear a tie.

Jordan avoided thinking about mushy stuff as much as he could, but sometimes he noticed Wade put his arm around Aunt Paulie and once he had seen them kissing, just like actors in a steamy music video. Except they were way too old for that.

Gross!

Finally Wade turned the truck onto a gravel road that seemed to go straight into the woods. Jordan looked around curiously, but he didn't see any buildings.

"Are there any wild animals around here?" he asked as they bumped over the deep ruts. Maybe they would see a bear or a mountain lion! He had seen a herd of elk once on the way to Sequim.

"There are probably lots of rabbits and a few deer," Wade replied, disappointing him. "One day I spotted a coyote when I was eating my lunch, but they're pretty skittish. And there's an eagle's nest in the top of an old dead tree called a spar. You can see it from the site."

Just then, the woods got thinner and Jordan could see the houses. One of them looked normal, but the other reminded him of a skeleton made out of wood. On the roof, a guy wearing a hard hat was on his hands and knees. He was making a *bang, bang, bang* noise.

"Wow." Jordan sat up straighter as he nearly forgot about the man he was going to meet. "They're right on the beach." A kid who lived here could have a tree house in the woods and a little sailboat for the water, too. There was even room for a horse if you fenced some of the flat, open part.

Wade pulled up next to two other trucks and a black Harley. Nearby stood a skinny little building made of plastic. Harold's Honey Buckets was printed on the door with a phone number under it. He knew it was like a portable bathroom, so the workers didn't have to run into the woods to take a leak.

"These places are going to be terrific when Steve's done," Wade said as he cut the engine. "His houses are pretty fancy."

Steve. Jordan swallowed hard at the reminder, but then a funny thing happened. His nervousness was replaced by curiosity. Ben, his best friend back home, had the same brown eyes and hooked nose as his dad. This would be Jordan's chance to find out if he looked like Steve. Even though his blond hair and blue eyes were a lot like his mom's, the idea that he could also resemble someone he'd never met was kind of weird.

Wade didn't immediately open his door. Instead he released his seat belt and shifted so that he was facing Jordan.

"You okay?" Wade asked.

Jordan had an idea of what the question really meant, even though he didn't have the nerve to ask right out if Wade knew whether or not Steve was his father. "You aren't going to say anything to him about, about—" he stammered, not ready to discuss it yet.

Wade shook his head. "Don't worry." He reached behind the seat and pulled out a file folder. "The only thing we're going to talk about today is houses, I promise."

Jordan felt a wave of relief, like after he had cleared a jump on his board without falling. It was pretty cool how Wade could almost read what he was thinking without him having to explain.

"Okay," Jordan agreed, unlocking his belt. "I'm ready."

"Looks like we won't need you to do the rough-in until the end of next week." As Steve talked to the electrician on his cell phone, he paced back and forth across the floor of the future kitchen. He barely heard the steady thunk of Carlos's nail gun overhead or the whine of George's saw.

"I'll get back to you on Monday," Steve promised the electrician as he noticed Wade's truck coming slowly down the drive. "Thanks."

After Steve had ended the call and stuffed the phone into his shirt pocket, he jotted a reminder to himself on his clipboard. The next two items on his punch list, calls to the cable outfit and the roofing supplier, could wait until after he took a break.

Steve flipped up the page and added another item to the second list he was writing: plan bachelor party. He didn't see Wade as the type who wanted a stripper, so he figured that something including bars and booze would work.

As soon as he saw the boy get out of Wade's truck with the sun shining down on his blond hair like some kind of spotlight, Steve froze. He knew instantly who the kid must be, so what the hell was Wade thinking to bring him here? Didn't Steve have enough to deal with?

Wade rested one hand on the boy's shoulder as they approached and gestured with the folder in his other hand at a red-tailed hawk making lazy circles overhead as it hunted for field mice in the tall grass.

As the boy made some comment, Steve studied him reluctantly. *Lily's child.* Except for the hair, sun-streaked like Steve's own, he looked like any other kid. He was a boy-man with gangly limbs and a self-conscious gait, stumbling awkwardly over a tuft of grass. His grin was destined to send pre-adolescent girls into fits of giggles. He was still too far away for Steve to be able to tell his eye color, but the resemblance to his mother was unmistakable.

Steve's chest ached as he watched the living reminder of his old fantasy, raising a family with Lily. From what he'd heard, she hadn't succeeded in finding the stardom she'd craved. Instead, she had ended up working as some kind of bookkeeper. Not very glamorous for someone with her talent and her dreams.

Not for the first time, he wondered just how she had managed, alone and pregnant at eighteen in such a tough town, no city for angels who were sweet and naive as she. Her beauty had been dazzling even then, so had she found an angel of her own to watch over her? To share her bed and pave her way?

The image of her as arm candy for some old

fart made Steve's stomach pitch. Deliberately he blocked out the silent questions. She had made her choice—and forced it on him, as well. Except for the boy who gazed up at him now, the whole sad story was ancient history.

"Hey, *amigo*," Carlos called down to Wade from his perch on the roof truss.

"Howdy, slackers." Wade's reply included George in his greeting. "Brought you some papers," he told Steve, holding out the folder.

"Oh?" Steve had no idea what it was about, unless it had something to do with Wade's wedding. Surely Steve wouldn't be expected to help with any decisions. He knew nothing about flowers or hymns. Reluctantly he stepped down to the ground and took the folder.

"This is my buddy, Jordan," Wade added in a breezy tone. "Lily's boy," he tacked on unnecessarily, if Steve was too dumb to see the resemblance—especially when he looked into eyes of the same blue that he saw in the mirror each morning.

Jordan's face turned pink. "Pleased to meet you," he mumbled, sticking out his hand despite his obvious embarrassment.

Steve pulled off his work glove and did the same. "Uh, you, too." He felt as awkward as a hooker in church as Jordan stuck his hands into the pockets of his baggy shorts and looked around.

"We're on our way to shoot some hoops," Wade drawled, breaking the silence. "Jordan wanted to see what a half-finished house looks like."

"Is that so?" Steve's doubt must have been evident, because Jordan's gaze darted from him to Wade.

Hell, none of this was the boy's fault. The least Steve could do was be civil.

"Well, come on, then," he said, ignoring Wade and the churning in his own gut. "I might as well give you the ten-cent tour. Ever use a nail gun?"

When Lily heard the familiar rumble of Wade's truck coming down the driveway alongside the big old house that she and Pauline had inherited from their parents, she slid a casserole dish into the oven and set the timer.

After "the guys" had left earlier, she had tried to search the Internet for office space to lease, but she had been unable to concentrate. Finally, she had given up in self-disgust. Cooking normally relaxed her, but not today. The entire time she'd been chopping onions, browning ground beef and boiling egg noodles, her thoughts had bounced back and forth between Pauline's recipe and her own brief glimpse of her first love.

Seeing Steve drive by had opened a floodgate of questions—uppermost being, what kind of man had he become and did he carry a grudge against her for the way she had left him?

When Jordan came into the kitchen moments later with Wade on his heels, she was in the act of transferring cooled brownies from a baking pan into a plastic container.

"Oh, wow!" Jordan exclaimed, reaching for one without bothering with a greeting. "My favorite."

Lily snatched them out of his reach. "You can say hello first, and then go wash your hands," she scolded.

Wade inhaled deeply. "But, Ma, we're starving."

"No exceptions," she said with a firm stare.

"Might as well do it," Jordan muttered, crossing to the sink. "She never gives in."

Lily set two of the fragrant brownies on paper napkins as they took turns with the kitchen towel. "Just one each so you don't spoil your appetites for dinner."

Lily and Jordan had been staying here with

Pauline, but on the first of the month they'd be moving into a small furnished house that Lily had sublet. Even though this grand old Victorian had more than enough room for all of them plus Pauline's boarder, Lily felt as though she and Jordan were imposing on the engaged couple's privacy. Besides, Lily wanted to be settled into a place of their own before school began in the fall and she opened her accounting office.

"Mom, guess where we went?" Jordan asked around a mouthful of brownie.

She glanced from him to Wade, who suddenly looked uncomfortable. "I thought you were going to shoot baskets at the park."

"We did," Wade replied, concentrating on his snack.

"I saw *two* houses being built right near the beach," Jordan continued. "Maybe we can buy one of them when it's done instead of renting that other little house."

"Oh?" Realization dawned on Lily, as clear and cold as a winter sunrise. She stared hard at Wade. "I doubt we'll be able to afford a house on the water," she muttered, a ball of anger and disbelief forming in her chest.

She wanted to yell at Wade, to demand to know what the hell gave him the right to make decisions for *her* son. To reach over and shake him by his broad shoulders until his shiny white teeth snapped together.

"How did you happen to go there?" she asked, keeping her voice calm with an effort that singed her throat.

Wade stared at the knife in her hand, the one she'd used to cut the brownies. "Jordan was curious," he said. "I didn't think it would be a big deal."

"Ah." Carefully Lily laid down the knife. "Jordan, since you're through eating, why don't you go up and change before dinner?" she suggested. "Maybe you should take a shower, too."

"Are you going to yell at Wade?" he asked.

"No," she replied truthfully, "I'm not going to yell at him." Maybe rip out his tongue with her bare hands or beat him silly with the wooden spoon she had used earlier.

Jordan hesitated. "Steve showed me how he and his crew were framing each room," he said defiantly, "and he told me I could come back again to see how it's going." His Adam's apple bobbed when he swallowed. "As long as it's okay with you."

Lily felt like a pot that might boil over at any second. "You and I will talk later," she told him firmly. "For now, please go ahead and do what I asked."

He ducked his head and left the room. "I liked him," he grumbled as he went through the dining room on his way to the foyer.

"What were you thinking?" Lily demanded of Wade through clenched teeth as soon as she heard her son's tread on the stairs. "You had no right to take him out there without discussing it with me first!"

Wade wiped his mouth with the napkin. "Good brownie," he murmured. "The kid's not deaf," he went on when she didn't respond. "He's heard all the speculation about Steve, so he was curious, that's all."

"And Jordan told you that?" she demanded, hurt that her own son would choose to confide in Wade instead of her.

A muscle jumped in Wade's cheek. "Well, not exactly, but I knew it had to bother him."

Wade's expression was defensive as he leaned his hip against the counter and folded his arms across his chest. "It was just a casual meeting, not a parent-child reunion," he added. "Nobody's making any big deal out of it except you."

When Lily continued to glare, he straightened again and threw his hands into the air in a gesture of defeat. "Look, if I overstepped, I'm sorry, okay?"

As an apology, it wasn't much, but she knew he genuinely cared about Jordan. Biting her lip, she stared out the kitchen window at the hollyhocks blooming along the fence in her sister's carefully tended backyard.

"I know you thought you were doing the right thing," she said softly, "and I appreciate that, but you don't understand the situation. It's complicated."

Wade rubbed a hand over his short black hair, his frustration obvious. The last thing she wanted was to alienate him, but neither could she allow her son to be hurt.

"No more visits to Steve without my permission," she added firmly. "Agreed?"

Wade started to argue, but then he must have thought better of it. "Okay," he replied with a solemn expression. "Still friends?"

Lily felt a wave of relief wash over her. "Of course."

After Wade went upstairs, she threw together a green salad to go with the casserole. When he came back downstairs and left to pick Pauline up from work, she went in search of Jordan.

Pauline's elderly boarder, Dolly Langley,

would be back from her cruise this evening, so Lily intended to take advantage of the temporary privacy.

She found Jordan curled up on the living-room couch with a library book, his hair still wet from his shower. He looked up when she sat down across from him.

"So you had a good day?" she asked hesitantly, wondering just how much to tell him.

He nodded, closing the library book, and looked at her with a wary expression. "Yeah."

"Want to tell me about it?" She felt as though she were walking through a mine field.

"I met Steve," he said, with an edge of defiance in his tone. "He showed me both the houses that he's building."

Steve must have been stunned when Wade presented Jordan to him. The conversation she owed him was one that she dreaded with a deep ache of regret. If she could only go back, but then she wouldn't have Jordan.

"Did Steve know about me?" he asked in a small voice. "I mean, before we came."

"No," she said truthfully. "I swear to you that he had no idea. Not even an inkling."

The tension drained out of his thin shoulders, making her realize he'd probably come to the conclusion that his father had ignored his existence for the past dozen years.

"Can I go see him again if he asks?" His expression was a mixture of longing and curiosity that nearly broke Lily's heart. At a total loss for words, she relied on the stock reply of parents everywhere for questions that had no answer.

"We'll see," she said, knowing she couldn't stall her son forever—and figuring it was one request that Steve would most likely never make. "We'll see."

Chapter Three

When Steve's doorbell rang on Saturday afternoon, the last person he expected to see standing on his front porch was Lily's son.

"Jordan!" Steve opened the door wider as his two dogs stood eagerly behind him. "What are you doing here?" Steve's house was a couple of miles outside of town on a narrow country road with very little traffic.

Jordan shifted from one foot to the other, obviously nervous. "I used my birthday money for a ride." He ducked his head, shoulders hunched.

Behind him Steve saw the local taxi leaving his driveway. At least the kid hadn't hitched his way out here.

"I probably shouldn't have come," Jordan mumbled, cheeks flushed, "but I need to talk to you about something."

Steve had a pretty good idea what he meant. "Since you're here, you might as well come on in." Realizing how unfriendly he must sound, he cleared his throat and tried again. "Uh, want something to eat? I was just about to make a couple of sandwiches."

The boy's face brightened immediately. "Yeah, that would be great." As soon as he crossed the threshold, the dogs approached him with their tails wagging.

Cautiously Jordan extended his hand. "What are their names?"

"The bigger one is Seahawk and that's Sonic," Steve said after he had shut the carved wood door.

"Are they watchdogs?" Jordan asked as they sniffed his fingers.

The idea of either of them going after a burglar made Steve smile. "Nah, they're golden retrievers. They love everybody."

He led the way past the living room with its massive rock fireplace and vaulted ceiling, down the hall through the family room where he'd been watching TV, and into the gourmet kitchen.

"Wow," Jordan exclaimed, head swiveling. "This place is way cool. Did you build it, too?"

"Yeah," Steve replied, pleased by the compliment. "I designed it and did most of the work."

After Jordan had wrapped his gangly legs around a bar stool at the granite center island and the dogs thumped down on the floor, Steve began pulling sandwich fixings from the stainless-steel double-door refrigerator.

"Does your mom know where you are?" he asked casually. Was she the kind of single parent who let her kid run wild while she was busy doing her own thing? He couldn't imagine her giving permission for him to come here.

Steve knew nothing about her, so he shouldn't jump to conclusions.

"Not really," Jordan replied.

Steve held up a container of mustard with a questioning glance. When Jordan nodded, he squirted it onto the bread. "Won't she be worried?" He doled out slices of ham and cheese as though he were dealing cards at a blackjack table, topped the stacks with lettuce and slapped on more bread.

Jordan looked longingly at the sandwiches, reminding Steve of the voraciousness of a growing boy's appetite. "She's looking at an office to rent and Dolly thinks that I walked over to the library," he said. "Mom lets me walk there by myself."

Steve put the sandwiches on plates and passed one over, impressed that Jordan didn't immediately dig in. After Steve had set out two cans of soda and torn open a bag of chips, he sat down, too. Only then did the kid finally begin to eat.

Steve debated called Pauline's house, then decided to hold off. It sounded as though Jordan had done a good job of covering his tracks. While they ate, Steve waited for him to start talking.

"Can I go out on the deck?" Jordan asked after he'd wolfed down the sandwich and taken a long swallow of soda.

"Sure," Steve replied. "Don't fall over the railing."

The house sat on a low bluff above the water with wooden steps leading down to the beach. On a clear day, he could see all way to Whidbey Island.

Letting the dogs outside, he joined Jordan at the rail. The deck hugged the back and one end of the house, so that part of it was shaded in the afternoon and the rest remained in the sun.

"See those dark things in the water?" Steve asked, pointing. "They're probably a pod of killer whales."

Jordan stared with his face scrunched up as the breeze off the water ruffled his thick hair. "Oh, yeah. I've seen pictures."

"So, what's on your mind?" Steve finally asked when the silence had lengthened between them.

Jordan looked up at him through eyes that stirred up long-buried memories of his mother. "One of the other kids told me that you're my dad," he said. "Is it true?"

Although he'd known the question was coming, Steve had no idea how to respond. "And what does your mom say?" he asked, stalling in case inspiration decided to visit him.

Jordan turned to stare out at the water. "All she's ever said was that you—uh, *he*, couldn't be with us. I figured she meant my dad was dead, like my friend's father who was a marine. I didn't want to make her feel sad, so I never asked anything more."

Silently Steve digested the information. No wonder Jordan had been willing to spend his money for a taxi to come all the way out here and confront him. The kid was filled with curiosity and he had no one to talk to about it. What the hell was Lily thinking? Even if the donor had been a one-night stand, she owed the kid some kind of explanation.

Steve rested his hand on one thin shoulder. "Tell you what," he said, hoping he was doing the right thing, "I'm going to take you home now, because your mom is the one who really needs to explain everything to you."

This mess was Lily's problem, but from what Steve could tell, she must have done a decent job of raising the boy. Somewhere along the way, she must have acquired the necessary parental instincts to handle difficult subjects like this. He, on the other hand, was clueless.

"She's going to be pissed at me," Jordan protested as Steve herded him back inside.

Steve let the word slide. "I think she'll understand." As he grabbed the keys to his pickup from a bowl by the front door, he tried to sound reassuring. "Besides, you're old enough to know the truth."

* * *

Lily hurried through the back door into Mayfield Manor, looking for someone to tell her exciting news to. After a week of fruitless searching, she'd met Wade and their real estate agent at a small house that had just recently been rezoned for commercial use. The one-story structure sat on a large corner lot near the courthouse in an older, well-maintained section of town. With some remodeling, it would be perfect for their offices: her CPA business and his investment firm.

As soon as Lily entered the large, updated kitchen in the old Victorian where she'd grown up, she became aware of the silence. Pauline was still at the shop, but Jordan should be here with Dolly, the boarder.

Frowning, Lily glanced at the small blackboard above the counter where messages had been left for as long as she could remember. Sure enough, something was written there in Dolly's spidery handwriting.

Jordan gone to library. Dolly taking nap.

Hands on her hips, Lily blew a lock of hair out of her eyes. She wished Dolly had indicated when he'd left.

Lily glanced at the clock above the stove, tempted to call Pauline. On Saturday afternoon the historic downtown shops and galleries would be full of tourists, so her news would have to wait. Meanwhile, Lily could start a list of all the things that would need to be done to the property if the seller accepted their offer.

At least financing her share wasn't one of them. Francis had provided generously for her and Jordan in his will. She blessed the day she'd met him at an open audition right after she first arrived in LA.

She divided the sheet of paper into columns: Exterior, Interior, Furniture and Equipment, she wrote across the top. They would need to order a sign, too. Maybe a native craftsman could carve one out of cedar, with classy gold lettering.

She hardly noticed the sound of an approaching truck until it slowed in front of the house. Glancing distractedly through the bay window, she expected Wade. What she saw instead made her leap to her feet as the notepad slid to the floor and the pen fell from her suddenly nerveless fingers.

Steve Lindstrom had parked his white pickup in the driveway. At first she assumed that he was looking for Wade, but as she watched from behind the swagged satin drapery, the passenger door opened and her son climbed out. Steve must have given him a ride home from the library.

Jordan started to dash across the front yard, only to skid to a halt when Steve called out to him. Lily was torn between staring at the tall, muscular man striding toward the front door and dashing to the gilt-framed wall mirror to check on her own appearance. Before she could decide, Jordan reached the porch.

Lily's feet refused to move. As she smoothed down her khaki skirt where it tended to wrinkle around her hips, the front door burst open. Her heart thumped with expectation as Jordan walked in, followed by the man she hadn't faced for thirteen years. The man she had loved with all her heart, even when she had walked out of his life without saying goodbye.

"Hello, Lily."

His voice was deeper than she remembered, and his smooth young face had matured and weathered into one that would turn any female's head. His sun-streaked hair was longer than she remembered as it fell across his forehead and brushed his collar. His intense blue eyes were more guarded. Below a mustache that added a rakish touch to his appearance, his mouth was curved into a smile that held neither warmth nor humor.

For the first time in her life, Lily forgot about her son until the sound of his voice reminded her of his presence.

"Steve brought me home," he said unnecessarily. There was a touch of belligerence in his tone that surprised her.

"I can see that," she replied, her gaze still on the man who seemed to fill the foyer with his presence. "It's been a long time."

His only response was to nod in agreement.

He had bulked up, she realized. His shoulders and arms looked even more powerful than during his days on the football team. If he experienced the slightest reaction to seeing her again, his expression hid it well. She, on the other hand, felt as though she might fly apart as emotions she'd thought long dead sizzled through her, threatening to choke off her air.

"It was nice of you to give my son a ride." She was grateful that her voice was rock steady as she glanced from one male to the other. "Didn't you find any books that you liked?" she asked when she finally noticed Jordan's empty arms. Usually he would check out anything he could find on dinosaurs or astronomy.

Sensing that her hands were shaking, she tucked them into her skirt pockets. To her surprise, Steve touched Jordan's shoulder in an obvious gesture of encouragement.

"I didn't run into Jordan at the library. He showed up at my house."

Lily couldn't have been more surprised if Steve had said they had run into each other at a quilting bee. "You hitched?" she demanded, horrified that he would break one of her biggest rules.

Jordan shook his head. "I took a taxi."

She didn't have to ask why. "And what did you tell him?" she demanded of Steve, hoping he hadn't been too callous. It wasn't as though he owed her the slightest atom of consideration, but Jordan was an innocent victim in this mess. One who had deserved to hear the truth from his mother a long time ago.

"He wouldn't tell me anything," Jordan replied before Steve could. "He said to ask you." His voice was accusing, as though he was fed up with being jerked around.

Lily's cheeks flamed with embarrassment. She had no one to blame but herself that this awkward conversation wasn't taking place in private. Before she could tell Steve how sorry she was that he had been drawn into it, he ruffled Jordan's hair.

"I'll see you, kid," Steve said. "Obviously you two have a lot to discuss, so I'd better go."

"Thanks for the sandwich," Jordan replied. "Your house is really cool, and so are your dogs."

The wistful note in her son's voice sent fresh guilt surging through Lily. All of this was her fault.

"Yes, thank you," she echoed as Steve walked out the front door. "It was, um, good to see you again."

He glanced back at her, one golden brow arched mockingly. "Right. You, too." His tone was dry. "Talk to your son," he added with a last glance at Jordan. "Take care."

"'Bye," Jordan replied.

Refusing to stare at Steve's retreating form, Lily shut the front door firmly while her mind spun in search of inspiration.

"Was that Steve?" Dolly asked from the landing at the top of the stairs. "He's such a nice young man, isn't he? A real hunk."

Dolly hadn't been living in Crescent Cove when Lily left, but no doubt she'd heard the story of Pauline's broken engagement to

Carter Black more than a decade ago, and the part Lily had played.

"He gave Jordan a ride," she said. "How was your nap?" She was tempted to use Dolly's appearance as an excuse to postpone the conversation she needed to have with her son, but she refused to take the coward's way out.

"I feel like a new woman," Dolly replied as she descended the stairs slowly with one gnarled hand on the carved wood banister. "I think I'll have a cup of tea and sit in the garden. Would either of you care to join me?"

"No, thanks," Jordan replied politely.

"Me, neither," Lily said. "There's something that my son and I need to discuss, so if you'll excuse us..." Her voice trailed off as she realized there was no going back now. After she answered Jordan's question about his paternity, she would need to talk to Pauline, as well. Lily could only hope that their recent reconciliation would be strong enough to handle the truth.

"We'll be in my room if you need anything," she added.

"Go ahead and have your chat." Dolly gave them a smile and a dismissing wave. "I've got a new mystery that I'm eager to read."

* * *

Steve drove straight from seeing Lily to his favorite watering hole down by the docks. The Crab Pot was a tavern with a big-screen TV, a couple of pool tables, decent food and a postage-size dance floor. This afternoon, the only thing that interested him was the cold beer on tap and the chance to sort out his reactions in familiar surroundings.

He pulled into the gravel parking lot, bouncing across the potholes, and parked near the worn steps leading past a row of weathered wood pilings to the peeling front door. Colorful neon beer signs lit up the window with a fishing net hanging across the top. He barely noticed any of it as he went inside.

He was greeted with the odors of deep-fried seafood and yeasty beer, the buzz of voices from the bar, music from the jukebox and the occasional snick of pool balls colliding with one another on a nearby table. Riley, the oversize member of the local Suquamish tribe who served as a bouncer, sat at the bar where he was deep in conversation with one of the waitresses.

Pausing in the doorway, Steve noticed Wade seated alone at a table. He glanced up from his newspaper and waved Steve over.

"Need a menu, honey?" asked the waitress, whose helmet of red hair was as familiar to Steve as the moose head mounted over the bar.

"No, thanks, Char," he replied. "Just bring us a fresh pitcher and another glass."

"What are you doing here in the middle of the day?" Wade asked as he put aside the paper. On the table sat a plastic basket holding a couple of lonely fries and an empty tartar sauce container.

Steve pulled out the chair opposite him and sat down. "I got thirsty. What's your story?"

Wade shrugged. "Pauline's at the shop and I found a new office, so I'm celebrating."

"Good for you. Where's it at?" Glad for the distraction, Steve listened carefully while Wade described the old house and his plans to renovate it. "Call me if you need any help," Steve offered when Wade had finally run down.

"Thanks," Wade replied. "What's new with you?"

Steve slouched down in the chair and stretched out his legs to the side. "Guess who showed up on my doorstep a while ago?"

Wade's forehead pleated into a puzzled frown. "I dunno. Who?"

Steve hesitated while Char brought over a pitcher of pale amber liquid. After filling his glass and topping off Wade's, she collected the lunch trash.

"Anything else I can bring you all right now?" She worked her gum, one hand parked on her hip. A pencil was stuck through the swirl of hair above her ear and a plastic name tag was pinned to the front of her red-and-black uniform shirt. "The mussel stew is real good today."

"No, thanks," Steve replied. If he tried to eat with his stomach churning like a concrete mixer, he would probably regret it.

"You were about to reveal the identity of your visitor," Wade prompted as soon as Char sauntered off with her tray tucked under one arm. "I hope it wasn't a process server slapping you with a lawsuit."

"Nothing like that," Steve replied after he'd wet his throat. "I'd almost prefer that it had been."

Wade's eyes widened. "Lily came to see you?" he guessed.

"Close enough." Steve wiped the foam from his mustache with a paper napkin. "Her son."

Wade muttered an expletive. "What did he want?"

"What do you think?" Wade didn't interrupt as Steve described the visit, right down to seeing Lily when he took Jordan home.

"She must have been as sweet as cotton candy back in high school," Wade commented with a shake of his head. "I'll deny it if you quote me, but she's sure as hell strike-me-blind gorgeous now."

"I suppose." Steve concentrated on making a row of wet rings on the tabletop with his glass. "Yeah, she was the prettiest girl in school, but she was really nice, too, you know? Not at all stuck-up, even though her folks treated her like a future Miss Universe."

"That's pretty much what Pauline told me," Wade replied. "That she was the brain and Lily the princess."

The girls' parents had been killed in a boating accident while Pauline was in college and Lily was a high-school student. Damn, but Steve didn't feel like discussing ancient history.

He drained his glass. "I was hoping Lily had changed, gotten hard-looking, I guess." He gave Wade a rueful grin. "With a couple of missing teeth, thinning hair, maybe a scar or a couple hundred pounds of added weight, you know?"

Wade laughed. "Didn't happen, man. She's hot."

"Yeah," Steve agreed reluctantly. If she had been the least bit affected by the sight of him, she'd hidden it well.

"Big reunion?" Wade teased after he'd swallowed some of his beer. "Hugs and kisses all around?"

"Yeah, right." Steve rolled his eyes as the tension binding his chest like steel bands began to ease up. "More like 'cool as you please and what have you been doing with my kid?'"

"*Her* kid?" Wade echoed, expression questioning. "Are you so sure that's all?"

For a moment, Steve was silent as regret, relief and a decades' old feeling of loss twisted together inside him like razor wire. "Positive," he said finally.

Wade's eyebrows spiked. Doubt flashed across his face, followed immediately by dawning understanding. "You never slept together."

Steve pointed his finger like a cocked pistol. "Give the man a prize." At this rate, he would have no secrets left.

"If he's not your son, then whose is he?" Wade asked, leaning across the table.

"Damned if I know," Steve admitted past

the sudden tightness gripping his throat. "Some guy she met down south, I guess, but she didn't tell me."

"That's not what everyone in town seems to have concluded," Wade said after Char had checked on them and left again. "You've got to admit the evidence is pretty compelling."

Steve snorted. "What, that he's got my coloring? Big deal."

"There's more to the argument than that." Wade shrugged. "Jordan's not deaf, obviously. So what did you tell him?"

"What could I say? I said for him to ask his mother." Steve poured another beer. He could always ask Wade to drive him home later.

"I'd like to be a fly on the wall during that conversation," Wade muttered as he raised his glass. "Here's to negative paternity test results."

If you only knew, Steve thought, touching his schooner to Wade's. "And to moving on."

Lily paced restlessly back and forth in her bedroom as she waited for Pauline to get home from work. Finding out that a cool guy—in her son's opinion—wasn't his father after all was going to be disappointing for a boy with a blooming case of hero worship.

She wanted to blame Wade for starting it, but she knew that wouldn't be fair. The wheels had been set into motion long before he'd decided to meddle. She should have talked to Jordan before they came back to Crescent Cove, but she hadn't wanted to add to his anger and grief. Nor had she realized how much gossip there would be—hadn't wanted to think their arrival would be such a reminder of her reason for fleeing in the first place.

As though it were yesterday, Lily could picture the shock on her sister's face when she walked into the library at the manor during the graduation party she'd thrown for Lily and seen Carter trying to kiss her. Pauline's fiancé and her sister. The betrayal had to hurt even more after Pauline had quit college to come home after their parents' accident so that Lily could finish high school here instead of being shipped off to some aunt she barely knew.

Lily knew now that Pauline had figured out that Carter had kissed her against her will. After Pauline had thrown her engagement ring in his face and the story got around, Lily had taken the coward's way out. At the time, she had truly believed it would spare both Pauline and Steve any more pain.

Seeing Lily again a few weeks ago had obviously reopened old wounds for Pauline, but because of her generosity and willingness to put the past behind them, she and Lily had found the way back to each other. Being close again was a dream come true for Lily.

Now she sat down on the edge of her bed with her hands covering her face. She hated the idea of bringing Pauline fresh pain, but she had no choice. It was time for the truth to come out. The whole truth.

If she was going to finally level with Jordan, she would also have to rip out her sister's heart.

Chapter Four

When Lily heard Pauline's SUV in the driveway, followed by the sounds of the back door opening and shutting, she stopped pacing restlessly in her bedroom. Heart thudding, Lily prayed silently for words that would minimize the fresh pain she was about to inflict on her sister.

No excuses, Lily reminded herself as she went downstairs. *No more secrets*. She had known this day would come, this conversation, and there was no one to blame for the reasons behind it except herself.

"Lily!" Pauline exclaimed when she walked through the archway separating the dining room from the foyer. "You look so serious. Is everything all right? Is Jordan okay?"

"He's fine," Lily replied with an automatic glance upward toward his room. After she'd told Jordan she would talk to him later, she asked him to stay in his room while she talked to his aunt. Dolly had gone to bingo and dinner with friends.

Pauline carried her purse and her laptop. "Did you meet with the real estate agent?" she asked. "Good news?"

After the later events of the day, Lily had nearly forgotten about finding the house. "Yes to both questions."

"Fantastic!" Pauline exclaimed. "From your gloomy expression, I thought it must not have worked out." She stuck out her foot. "Give me five minutes to get out of these shoes and visit the bathroom. I'll be back down in a minute to hear all about it, okay?"

Lily was grateful for the respite. "Want some lemonade?"

Pauline was already halfway up the stairs. "Sounds good," she called over her shoulder.

When she came back down a few minutes later, Lily had set two full glasses on a tray and carried it into the library, where she could shut the heavy walnut door and they wouldn't be disturbed. The room with its walls of book-shelves and tiled fireplace had always been one of Pauline's favorites.

"Let's go outside," she suggested. "It's nice in the backyard." With her fondness for gardening, she had created a small Victorian paradise of traditional plantings there, along with a seating area complete with a gazing ball that rested on a pedestal.

Lily set the tray on their father's massive carved desk and turned to face her sister. "Not right now," she replied. "There's something I need to tell you without being interrupted."

Pauline's smile faded. "You aren't going back to California, are you?" she asked. "It's been wonderful having you and Jordan here."

"No, that's not it." Lily took her lemonade and sat down on one of the maroon velvet settees that flanked the empty fireplace. Her hand shook, rattling the ice against the glass, so she set it on a coaster on a side table and crossed her legs.

"You may want me to leave when I'm done talking," she added sadly. What could she have been thinking, all those years ago, that had brought them to this now?

Pauline sat on the matching settee. "You're scaring me, Liliput." She hadn't used that nickname since way before Lily had moved to LA.

"Jordan took a taxi out to Steve's house this afternoon," Lily said around the lump of nerves in her throat.

"What?" Clearly the news came as a shock to Pauline. She leaned forward. "Tell me what happened."

Briefly Lily related how Steve had brought him home. "I need to tell him that Steve isn't his father," she continued, "but I wanted to talk to you first."

"I should have known that you wouldn't have kept Steve in the dark if he had a son," Pauline replied with a faint smile. "You don't have to say anything more if you don't want to. What happened in LA is your business, after all."

The temptation to grasp at the branch Pauline extended was nearly overwhelming. Lily wavered for a moment, but then she pressed on. "Paulie," she said softly, "I do need to tell you because you have a right to know the truth."

As Lily reached for her glass and took a sip of lemonade, Pauline's hazel eyes widened.

"Why is that?" she asked warily, sitting up straighter. "Tell me."

Tears filled Lily's eyes, blurring her vision.

"I never meant it to happen," she said through trembling lips. "I'm so sorry." She swallowed hard. "It was Carter. He's Jordan's father."

"How…?" Pauline asked. "Oh, my God, Lily. Did he rape you?"

For a moment, Lily was tempted to say that he had. There was no one to refute her if she did, since Pauline's ex-fiancé was dead, killed in a car accident a few years ago.

Lily hung her head. "No, it wasn't rape," she admitted softly. "I guess you'd call it seduction, since he seemed to know just how to flatter me, to play me and make me think…" She shook her head. "No, I'm not going to make excuses. He pursued me and I… I just didn't say no."

The silence lengthened as her confession lay between her and Pauline like a rotting corpse. Lily wiped her eyes with her fingertips, only to see that tears were also running down her sister's cheeks, which were as pale as the alabaster vase on the fireplace mantel.

"You and Carter?" Pauline whispered hoarsely. "You *slept* with my fiancé?" Her gaze sliced through Lily like a knife. "I quit college to raise you," Pauline continued, hand pressed to her heart. "I even threw you a graduation party." Biting her lip, she shook her head slowly back and forth as though she was having trouble comprehending what Lily had told her.

"Paulie, I'm sorry," Lily said again, wishing there was some way she could make it all go away. Wishing there hadn't been a reason to ever confess to her own betrayal.

"You had Steve," Pauline continued, waving her hand. "He adored you. If he wasn't enough, you could have had anyone else you wanted, yet you took the man I loved. The one man who loved *me*." Her voice had risen, making Lily glad she'd shut the heavy door earlier.

"Will you just listen for a minute?" Lily pleaded. "Let me try to explain."

"How many times?" Pauline demanded. Her expression was grim as she got to her feet and began to pace. "How many times did you *do it* with him?" She leaned down so that her angry face was close to Lily's. "Was it here in this house that the two of you…?" She spun away, yanking a tissue from an enameled box on the end table.

"It was only once, I swear," Lily cried. She lowered her voice, aware of Jordan upstairs. "It's no excuse, I know. There is no possible justification for what I did, but I was eighteen.

Steve and I had been fighting a lot about his plans to play college football."

Pauline still glared, but at least she appeared to be listening.

"He'd canceled several dates with me so that he could go and talk to recruiters," Lily said rapidly. "It sounds so shallow, I know, but I was scared to death of losing him. Every time your back was turned, Carter would heap compliments on me, whispering in my ear how Steve didn't appreciate me, that he was only a boy and I deserved a man."

Pauline's eyes were red, but her tears had stopped flowing. "What about me?" she asked in an icy voice. "Did either of you even remember that I existed?"

Lily gulped back a fresh sob. Repeating what Carter had said was difficult. "He said you wouldn't sleep with him," she mumbled, staring down at her clasped hands. "That you wanted to wait, but he had needs. Needs that a real woman like me would understand." She laughed without humor, painfully aware of how he'd manipulated her. "Then Steve went over to WSU. He called me from a party the team hosted." She could almost taste the fear she'd felt. "I could hear girls in the background and he said he was having a blast."

"Was that when it happened?" Pauline asked.

Lily nodded. "You had gone to Seattle overnight with a girlfriend to see someone in concert, I think. I don't remember who, but Carter didn't want to go."

"It was a musical at the Fifth Avenue," Pauline recalled tonelessly, sitting back down so they were facing each other again. "It was *Cats*. He didn't care about seeing it, so Margo Lynn and I went together. We had dinner at the Palomino and shared a room at the Hilton." She leaned her forehead against her hand. "He and I argued about it beforehand. I remember—" She swallowed. "I remember telling myself that I was being selfish, just like he said, and that I needed to try harder to make him happy."

"I always felt so stupid around you," Lily continued anxiously, "just an empty-headed twit who could never hope to make the grades you did or go to college." She made a meaningless gesture with her hand. "He listened to me and asked my opinion about things. You remember how you and I talked after I first got home about how we both felt, growing up." She searched her sister's face, looking for a glimmer of understanding, but Pauline's set expression, lips pressed together in a straight line, revealed nothing.

"Mom was always dressing me up or styling my hair while Daddy read the newspaper to you or talked about all the choices you would have about what you wanted to be." Lily swallowed hard. "One time I said I wanted to be a scientist and they both laughed. Mom said my job would be to land a rich husband who could support all of us. I worried about what would become of me when I wasn't pretty anymore."

Pauline looked away, as though she didn't want to hear it.

From the corner, an elaborately carved grandfather clock chimed the hour. Lily could remember when their mother had brought it home as a birthday gift for their father.

"I'm not a grandfather yet," he'd said with a meaningful glance at Lily. "Not for a few more years." She had taken the remark not as a warning to behave herself, but as a reminder that her only aspiration should be marriage and babies. Pauline was the one with the brains for a career, not Lily.

"Anyway," she concluded, not knowing what else she could say in her own defense, "I knew that I owed you the truth before I tell Jordan."

"He's just a child. How are you going to make him understand?" Pauline asked.

Lily shrugged. "I haven't figured that out, but certainly not more than he's old enough to understand. It would only confuse him."

She looked down at her hands, clasped tightly in her lap. "And I can only guess how Steve feels with everyone looking at him sideways and whispering behind his back."

"Yeah, that's true," Pauline agreed. "Have you talked to him?"

"Just a polite exchange when he brought Jordan home today. It's the first time I've really seen him." Lily knew she owed Steve an apology, even though she couldn't admit the truth. He was someone else she had let down badly. The list seemed to be growing: Pauline, Jordan and now Steve. Who was next?

Impulsively, Lily leaned forward to touch her sister's hand, but then she stopped herself. "Can we get past this?" Her voice wasn't quite steady. "Do you need some time? Do you want me to leave, to take Jordan to a motel until the sublet is ready for us to move in?"

Pauline got to her feet. "I don't know," she replied. "This has come as a bit of a shock. I'd gotten my brain around the idea that Carter kissed you at your party and you tried to push

him away, but I never dreamed… I never…"
She bit her lip, but her hazel eyes finally met
Lily's. "What would you tell Jordan if you
had to go to a motel?"

Lily shook her head helplessly. "I'd think
of something." God, what *would* she tell him?
He was a smart boy and he would see through
a puny excuse.

Pauline let out a sigh. "Look, I know you
can't very well leave, but I do need to absorb
all this. Then we'll have to talk some more."

Her comment infused Lily with a feeling
of hope she didn't deserve. Another flood of
tears blurred her vision. "That's fine. I understand." Her lip quivered. "Anything you
say, just…" She didn't know what else to add.
"I'm sorry," she repeated, her new mantra.
She was well aware of how woefully inade-
quate her apologies must sound by now.

Pauline didn't reply as she grabbed another
tissue. Blotting her eyes, she opened the door,
straightened her shoulders and left the library.
Watching her go, Lily released a long, slow
breath, surprised that, as well as burning eyes
and an aching tightness in her chest, she also
felt as though a huge weight had been lifted.

If only Paulie would be able to find it in her
heart to forgive her sister once again for hurt-

ing her—that was the sixty-four-thousand-dollar question.

Putting it aside, she squared her own shoulders and went slowly upstairs to her son's room.

Jordan was rereading the first Harry Potter book when there was a knock at his door.

"Who is it?" he asked without lifting his gaze.

His mom opened the door and poked in her head. "Can I talk to you?" she asked.

He figured she was going to chew him out about going to Steve's without asking first, but she didn't appear angry. She looked worried, her voice kind of quiet.

He tossed the book aside and sat up straighter, bracing himself and wishing he'd picked up his dirty clothes like she kept telling him to do. If for some bizarre reason she wasn't already mad, she might get that way when she looked around. Nervously he waited while she moved his jacket from the chair by his desk and sat down.

"There's something I probably should have told you a long time ago," she said, looking down instead of at him. "I guess I didn't know how to bring it up."

"I already know that Steve is my dad," he

said. "It's okay, Mom. He's pretty cool." Maybe he would let Jordan go out there again and play with the dogs.

She frowned, but she still didn't look mad. "I'm sorry, sweetie, but you're wrong. Steve isn't your father."

Disappointment was like a punch to his stomach. He had to blink to keep from crying like a little kid. "Are you *sure*?" he asked. He knew that Steve had been her boyfriend, but beyond that, his knowledge was a little blurry.

Her smile was sad, like when his hamster had died and they'd buried it in a shoe box. "Your father died a long time ago," she said, confirming his earlier assumption. "He never knew about you."

"Was he in the marines?" Jordan asked. "Was he a hero?"

An expression he couldn't read crossed her face. "No, he wasn't in the service." She took Jordan's hand in hers. "I want you to remember one thing, okay?" she said, using the same tone she always did when it was something really important, like when she had talked to him about being careful of strangers who might try to talk to him. "He would have been really, really proud of you, just like I am."

"What was his name?" Jordan asked.

She blinked and looked away. "John," she said softly. "His name was John."

After his mom had given him a hug and asked if he was okay, told him that dinner would be ready in a little while and left the room, he lay on the bed for a while before going back to his book. He still wished that Steve was his father, but Wade wasn't his dad and he spent time with Jordan. Maybe if Steve got to know him better, and liked him, he would do the same.

The one thing that bothered him was the way she had acted when he asked his dad's name. If she wasn't his mom, he might have thought she was lying.

"John." He said the name aloud, trying it out. "My father's name was John."

Steve hadn't drunk nearly enough beer at the Crab Pot to scrub Lily's image from the inside of his skull when Wade's cell phone rang.

"Sorry, old man." Wade shifted in his chair in order to retrieve it. "Forgot to turn the damn thing off." He peered at the screen. "It's from Pauline's house," he added. "She thought she might work late, but maybe she changed her mind. I'd better take it."

When Steve nodded, he realized that he

did have a bit of a buzz. Testing himself, he topped off both their schooners with a hand that shook more than he'd expected. *What the hell*, he decided as he took a long drink. Normally, he didn't overindulge, but today he'd earned it with a teasing little taste of how having a son of his own might feel.

"Why do you want to know?" Wade asked, speaking quietly into his phone.

Steve eavesdropped unashamedly as Wade's glance met his and then veered away. "Well, to tell the truth, he happens to be sitting right here with me."

"Who?" Steve questioned silently. If it was a subcontractor with a problem, he didn't want to hear it, but he couldn't imagine why they would call Wade instead of him.

Wade mouthed something silently, but Steve was no lip-reader. "I don't know if this is the best time," Wade said into the phone.

"Time for what?" Steve forgot to whisper and Wade rolled his eyes.

"Yeah, that was him," he confirmed, staring intently at Steve. "Hold on for a minute."

Resigned, Steve tried to take the phone, but Wade held it out of his reach and then he put his free hand over the mouthpiece.

"It's Lily," Wade said softly. "She wants to come down here and talk to you."

"Lily?" Steve echoed, his nice little buzz disappearing. "What the hell does she want?" he whined.

Wade shrugged. "She said she needs to see you about something and it can't wait."

Maybe seeing him this afternoon had made her realize what a huge mistake she'd made thirteen years ago. Yeah, and maybe one of his dogs would sign a recording contract and make him rich.

He slapped his hands down on the table. "Bring her on," he invited with a burst of bravado.

"You sober enough to deal with her?" Wade asked.

"Sober enough, stupid enough, it's all the same to me," Steve replied, gesturing with reckless abandon. "Let's see what the little lady has to say for herself."

Wade appeared less than convinced, but he told Lily where they were. Steve shoved aside his beer and waved Char over to order some coffee. Despite the questions he might like answered, there was only one subject he could think of that Lily might want to discuss with him and that was Jordan.

"She's coming straight down," Wade said as he shoved back his chair. "There's a table open, so let's rack up a game while you're waiting."

It sure beat sitting on his thumbs with a pulse beating in his head like a hammer, Steve figured, even if it cost him twenty bucks. Silently he lurched to his feet and followed his friend.

While Wade ran the table on him with humiliating ease, Steve slapped down his money and gulped the coffee Char brought him. He hoped the caffeine would give him a needed jolt. They had just sat back down when Lily walked into the tavern.

She looked like a supermodel, lean and leggy in a cropped green top above snug jeans and high-heeled sandals. The sudden silence at the bar was punctuated by a low whistle which she ignored as she glanced around the room. Steve gawked like a groupie while Wade stuck up his hand to get her attention.

"Hey, Lily!" he called.

Cheeks flushed, she came toward them with her perfect breasts bouncing gently. How Steve wished she had somehow lost the ability to make the blood drain from his head and the spit dry up in his mouth. The truth was that she still got to him on an elemental male level and the damn coffee hadn't helped him one little bit.

When she stopped at their table, her white-knuckled grip on the strap of her shoulder-bag was the only sign that she might be nervous.

"Hi," Wade said, getting politely to his feet.

Belatedly, Steve followed. His mother's voice was in his head, scolding him as though she were standing next to him instead of on some golf course in Arizona where she and his father had retired years ago.

"Hi, guys." Lily's gaze included them both.

"Come on, sit down," invited Wade, their self-appointed host, as he dragged over a chair from the next table.

"Thanks." She didn't move, biting her lip as she looked more fully at Steve. He was reminded with painful clarity of just how he used to feel when she linked her arm through his and smiled up at him—as if he were the king of the world. Now, though, for a fraction of an instant, he merely felt like a loser.

The knee-jerk reaction was followed immediately by a burst of irritation that he had allowed her to slip past his defenses so easily. Where was a man's pride when he needed it the most?

"Um, actually I need to talk to you in private," she said hesitantly, surprising him. "Could you come outside for a few minutes?"

His first impulse was to refuse, but it wasn't in his nature to be outright rude. Besides, his reaction to her presence wasn't her problem—it was his. Most of the men in this town would treat an invitation to go outside with Lily as something akin to free Superbowl tickets, not to be turned down unless you'd lost your mind.

"I'll be back," he told Wade.

Wade sat down and lifted his glass in a toast. "I'll be here." He winked at Lily. "See you later."

"Thanks," she replied with a faint smile before she led the way toward the entrance and the parking lot beyond.

"Hey, Lindstrom," called out one of the patrons seated at the bar, "how'd you get so lucky twice in your lifetime?"

Ignoring him, Steve held open the front door and then followed her outside. The sky was filled with light gray clouds and a mild wind had sprung up, but it wasn't cold. As he trailed after her down the wood steps, he couldn't help noticing that her denim-clad bottom had ripened deliciously, begging for the touch of a man's hands. Her waist was just as slim as he remembered. The hair falling to her shoulders was still a stunning mixture of silver and gold, several shades lighter than Pauline's, and the scent that floated back to him was a painful reminder of all the times he had held her in his arms while they planned their future together.

He could hardly believe that she hadn't changed perfumes in all this time.

He was trying to regain his objectivity when she stopped in the middle of the gravel pathway and turned so abruptly that he nearly ran her down. Despite the high heels on her sandals, she still had to look up at him.

"Do you want to sit in my car?" she asked, arms folded across her chest.

In a confined space, her nearness was bound to send him over the edge. "No," he exclaimed, causing her eyes to widen. "Uh, let's sit on that old bench by the water."

The tavern had been built long before a good view mattered, so the back of the low-slung structure had only a couple of small windows at the far end.

"That would be fine," she replied softly.

Automatically, he reached for her elbow in order to escort her over the gravel, but she hurried on ahead of him, reminding him that she no longer needed his assistance and hadn't for years.

She sat at one end of the bench and he took the other, facing her. Despite the popularity of the nearby fishing dock, there was no one else in sight. Was he finally going to get the explanation that had plagued him for years?

"I owe you an apology," she said bluntly. "There was a lot more that I wanted to say when you brought my son home, but I needed to talk to him first."

"I understand." Steve's earlier suspicion, that she wanted to discuss the rumors about Jordan's parentage, was confirmed. He felt a surprisingly sharp pang of disappointment. What had he expected, that she was about to declare her undying love?

He ignored the vision of her that came to mind, on her knees at his feet as she begged him to take her back. "He seems like a good kid. How's he doing?" he asked.

Her face mirrored a mother's concern. "He's confused, of course. Being twelve, he sort of grasps the issues, but there's a lot that he's just too young to understand until he's older." She clasped her hands tightly on her lap. "I appreciate your not saying anything before you brought him home."

Steve shrugged. "You and I both know that it wasn't my call."

Her lips tightened and she looked away as the breeze off the water stirred her hair. He had always loved to run his hands through the silken strands and to bury his face in it.

"I'm sorry for any discomfort that I caused you," she said in a tight little voice. "It wasn't fair."

Gawd, but this was difficult. He'd thought he had outgrown her long ago, but right now the need to touch her was almost overwhelming. Angry with himself, he tried to ignore his rampaging hormones and pay attention to the subject at hand.

The boy he hadn't fathered.

"Nothing that happened back then was fair," he agreed. "Why did you leave without saying goodbye?" The question had haunted him for years.

Lily closed her eyes, squeezing a lone tear from under her long, thick lashes. Refusing to be distracted by the blatant attempt at manipulation, he watched it trickle down her delicately molded cheek. A memory surfaced of him kissing away her tears after a hurtful comment by another cheerleader, but he shoved it ruthlessly aside.

"All that was a long time ago," she said finally. "There's no point in going into it now."

Her reply sent a burst of frustration roaring through him. "No point," he growled. *"No point?"*

Without conscious thought, he reached out and wrapped his hands around her upper arms, pulling her closer so they were almost nose to nose. "Trying to figure out *the point* was all I thought about for a hell of a long time," he grated through clenched teeth. "Don't you dare sit there like some overpromoted celebrity and tell me that explaining yourself to a dumb hick like me just isn't worth the effort."

She stared at him wide-eyed, her lips parted in obvious shock. Maybe he wasn't being entirely fair, but she had no right to blow him off when he wanted, no *needed*, a few answers. She had ripped out his heart and stomped on it.

Why, why, *why*?

"L-let me go, please," she stammered, chin quivering.

Realizing slowly that he was acting like the kind of bully he normally despised and that he'd no doubt succeeded in scaring the hell out of her, he figured that he had nothing left to lose.

Giving in to the temptation that had been riding him since she walked into the Crab Pot, he leaned down and kissed her.

Chapter Five

Steve's hands were wrapped around the bare skin of Lily's upper arms like twin vices. When his mouth covered hers, her whole body stiffened with shock. She intended to jerk away, then vaporize him with a blistering retort. As though he was able to anticipate her intention, he slid one hand up her throat to cradle her jaw. He changed the angle of the kiss, the soft sweep of his mustache caressing her skin before he nudged her lips apart with his tongue.

His work-roughened thumb caressed her chin while his familiar scent and taste stirred a passion she thought she'd succeeded in putting behind her. Unable to resist the feelings bubbling up inside her, she twisted in his embrace so that she could link her arms around his neck. Her breasts flattened against his hard chest. With her fingers tangled in his shaggy hair, she returned the kiss with wild abandonment.

He made a sound of triumph deep in his throat as his fingers tightened on her chin and he took the kiss to another level. His satisfied groan hit her like a pail of cold water, chilling her to the bone. What had she been thinking?

Horrified by the ease of her own capitulation, she jerked back, breaking his loose hold, and leaped to her feet. "What do you think you're doing?" she sputtered, cheeks flaming, body still tingling with reawaked desire.

As his glazed expression was immediately replaced by a hard, narrow-eyed stare, she wiped her arm across her lips as though she could somehow obliterate the scorching brand of his mouth on hers.

Her implied insult hit its mark as his face darkened and he stood up to tower over her. "I'm not going to apologize." His gaze bored into hers, his eyes burning with blue fire. "Not when it's so damned obvious just how badly you needed kissing."

His comment infuriated her, partly because

it was true. "Maybe so, but not by you," she shot back at him, hugging herself with her arms to keep from shaking.

"Did the men in California fall out of favor with your *discriminating* standards?" he all but sneered. "I'm surprised."

Ignoring the stab of pain as the insult sank in, she raised her chin. "Quite the opposite. My son and I found a wonderful man," she replied coldly. "If he hadn't died unexpectedly, we would still be with him."

She saw the shock darken his eyes before he screened them with his short, thick lashes. "Geez, Lily, I'm sorry," he said softly, his anger gone. "I had no idea."

She ignored his outstretched hand and his apparent remorse. "Why would you?" she snapped. "You don't know me. Frankly, after your display of macho-man brutality, I'd just as soon keep it that way." She knew that her accusation was unfair; she'd been with him all the way in that kiss. If she didn't make her escape, she was likely to do something even more stupid than returning his kiss, like crying or throwing herself into his muscular embrace. "Stay away from me and my son."

Knees shaking, she turned and walked quickly around the corner of the building.

Not until she reached her car did she risk a glance over her shoulder, but Steve was nowhere in sight. Telling herself that she hoped he had jumped into the bay, she fumbled with the lock and finally slid behind the wheel.

Two men getting out of a nearby SUV looked at her curiously. Ignoring them, she left the parking lot as fast as the potholes would allow. On her way back to Pauline's, she pounded the steering wheel with frustration. Instead of acting like a love-starved groupie, she should have slapped his arrogant face.

At least then she wouldn't have to contend with the aching reminder of how it felt to be back in his arms.

For the next couple of weeks, Steve did everything he could to physically exhaust himself each day before he went home. He spent so much time cutting boards and working side by side with his crew that Carlos finally complained that Steve kept getting in their way. He contacted the decorator so often that she stopped taking his calls. The flooring contractor nearly walked off the job and the real estate agent handling his listings—who'd been a buddy since high school—threatened to quit after telling Steve with a finger in his face that he needed to get laid.

Mark was probably right, Steve realized on his way home from their meeting. Too bad he was too fixated on the memory of kissing Lily to work up any real interest in mindless sex with anyone else.

What he craved was mindless sex with Lily.

Meanwhile, running his business into the ground and alienating his network of associates was getting him nowhere. Each morning he woke with the memory of that hot, sweet burst of heat throbbing through him like a jackhammer. At night, when he was finally able to grab a few hours of restless sleep, she invaded his dreams with X-rated scenarios he could never quite remember.

He was a wreck.

After he gotten home after another long, trying day and fed the dogs, who never failed to greet him with unbridled approval, he collapsed into a deck chair with a bottle of beer and the view for company. Since he doubted Lily would agree to Mark's suggestion, he'd have to switch to plan B.

Draining half the beer, he patted first Sonic's and then Seahawk's silky head as the two retrievers jostled jealously for position. Each repeatedly bumped his hand, licked his fingers and whined in a bid for attention.

"Settle down, you guys," Steve told them absently. When they ignored him, he repeated himself more firmly.

As if they sensed this was no time for playing around, their bodies hit the deck with twin thumps. He knew without looking that they were stretched out with their heads propped on their front paws, brown eyes fixated as they waited for their daily romp through the field.

Instead, he stared morosely at the smooth water and colorless sky. Sunset was the one time of day that he missed a western exposure with its streaks of purple and rose pink, and the red ball of a dying sun that disappeared into the Pacific.

Steve held his empty beer bottle to his temple as a headache began to throb there. Finally he set it next to his chair and got to his feet, intending to take the dogs for their run before it was too dark to see.

His cell phone rang cheerfully from the dining-room table where he'd tossed it earlier in a fit of disgust. His first impulse was to ignore it, but it might be business and he had two houses to sell.

"Hold the thought, guys," he told the dogs as he slid open the screen door and went inside. "Hey, Wade," he said after he'd checked the screen. Instantly his spirits lifted. "What's up?"

"Lily and I signed the papers." Wade's voice rang with enthusiasm. "It looks as though we bought ourselves an office."

"Is she there now?" Steve asked before he could stop himself.

"I'm at the house and she's upstairs putting Jordan to bed," Wade replied. "Why?"

"No reason." Steve felt foolish for asking, but at least he could count on Wade not to tell her. "Congratulations, man," he said. "I suppose now you'll want to start on the renovations."

"You bet." Wade chuckled. "You want to see the place before I tear it apart? I could use your input before I start the demo."

"Sure thing." Mentally, Steve reviewed his schedule. "How's tomorrow morning around eleven? I'll take an early lunch break."

He could hear Pauline's muffled voice before Wade came back on the line. "Perfect. Got a pen? I'll meet you there."

Steve jotted down the address. "See you in the morning." After he ended the call, he took his restless dogs for a walk along the bluff while he wondered if Lily had ever said anything about kissing him. Like it or not, he was bound to run into her around Wade and Pauline. He couldn't very well grab Lily every time she frustrated him, so he had better figure out a better way to handle the situation.

As soon as Wade and Jordan had left for the video store to rent a movie, Lily ducked out to the garage where the boxes she'd had brought up from California were stored. When she and Wade had gotten home from signing the papers on their building, Pauline, Dolly and Jordan had toasted their success.

Now, Dolly was watching a TV show from England in her room and Pauline had gone out front to water the flowerpots on the porch. Lily couldn't help but wonder if her sister was having second thoughts about Wade sharing an office with Lily, but neither of them had given any indication. She could only hope that Pauline knew that Lily would never betray her again.

Since she had first told Pauline about Carter, they hadn't discussed it again, even though Pauline treated her normally enough in front of the others. She figured that Pauline deserved some time to deal with Lily's latest bomb-shell, but she hoped her sister would give her some clue to her feelings before Lily and Jordan moved out next week. Lily wasn't even sure if Pauline still wanted her help with the wedding.

Since the house Lily had sublet was fully furnished, she wouldn't have to buy much until she was ready to purchase a place with some of the money that Francis had left her. Meanwhile, she wanted to see what pots and pans she'd brought with her. There had been so much to sort through and dispose of after Francis died that she honestly couldn't remember.

After she had switched on the light that hung from the ceiling of the remodeled carriage house, she studied the cardboard cartons that the movers had left stacked on the concrete floor. Each was labeled with its contents in her own handwriting.

A sudden wave of emotion caught her unprepared as she stared at the only remaining evidence of her life with Francis after he'd taken her in, pregnant and alone.

"Do you have a minute?"

The sound of Pauline's voice from the doorway startled Lily from her reverie. "Uh, sure,"

Lily replied, dabbing at her eyes before she turned around. "I thought you were out front."

"I figured it would be a good chance for us to talk undisturbed, if you have time." Pauline's expression was so solemn that Lily's hopes took a serious nosedive.

"Of course I do," Lily replied, glancing around for somewhere to sit. Her boxes weren't the only items stored in the garage; in the back corner was some furniture and other things that had belonged to their parents. Leaving the side door open so they could hear Wade's return, Pauline removed the sheets from two old steamer trunks.

"Care to join me?" she asked, gesturing with one hand.

Silently Lily walked over and sat down, heart pounding in her chest.

"I should have brought out some wine," Pauline said unexpectedly. "Someday, if it ever gets any easier, we'll have to go through this stuff and figure out what we want to keep."

Lily struggled not to fidget. "I suppose."

A car drove past the house with the bass from its music throbbing.

"The stuff is yours, too," Pauline continued. "If there's anything you want for your house or that you think Jordan might want someday…" Her voice trailed off and she shrugged. "Feel free."

"Thanks." The butterflies in Lily's stomach weren't content to flutter; they were dive-bombing. "I probably should save a few things for him." She was grateful that her sister wasn't the type of person to blame him for what had happened.

"He's a nice boy," Pauline said. "You've done a good job with him."

Her comment brought fresh tears to Lily's eyes. "Thank you," she whispered, ducking her head. "It's very generous of you to say that, especially under the circumstances."

"I told Wade," Pauline said. "We don't keep secrets. Steve may be his friend, but I trust him not to say anything."

Lily should have realized that Pauline would confide in her fiancé. My God, what must he think of Lily, now that he knew what she had done to the woman he loved?

"He must despise me," she whispered.

"It was Wade who made me see how wrong Carter was for taking advantage of you. He's the one who deserves most of the blame for what happened, not you," Pauline said softly, leaning toward Lily.

Lily's head shot up so she could look into Pauline's hazel eyes. "But I already told you that he didn't rape me," she said, voice breaking. "You couldn't have loved a rapist."

"He seduced you," Pauline corrected her firmly, "and he was the adult."

"I wasn't a child," Lily protested without thinking. "I really thought I knew what I was doing."

Pauline smiled faintly. "We'd both been through the trauma of losing Mom and Daddy just two years before." She clasped her hands together in her lap. "There's one thing that keeps nagging at me and I can't seem to get past it. How did Carter justify wanting you when he was supposedly in love with me?"

Pauline had zeroed in on the one thing that Lily would never, never reveal to her or to anyone else. Carter had admitted that he thought Pauline had enough insurance money to set up his legal practice.

The memory of his smug expression when he'd told her nearly made Lily sick. How could she have ever been foolish enough—and needy enough—to swallow his lies and believe his cheap flattery? And what to tell Pauline now?

"It started out with a little harmless flirting," she said hesitantly. "I admit to being flattered that an older man would notice me. In my mind, I kept it separate from his relationship with you." She swallowed. "It must sound so stupid now."

Pauline shook her head as though to encourage her to go on.

Lily licked her dry lips. "It seemed that Steve was always practicing and working out. Carter kept telling me how I deserved someone who would put me first." She took a deep breath. "I guess I got a crush on him, but I never intended doing anything about it, I swear."

"I understand," Pauline whispered. Her eyes were huge in her face.

Lily was torn between making her sister understand and not hurting her further. "He offered to come by and check on me when you had gone to the concert. He brought some wine and one thing led to another."

Pauline squeezed her eyes shut. "Go on," she insisted. "I want to know the rest."

The muscles in Lily's throat were so tight that it felt as though someone were choking off her air. "We kissed a few times. Then he said a man can't just…that he couldn't stop and that I had to follow through with what I'd started." She searched Pauline's averted face for some clue to her feelings. "I'm not trying to make excuses, because he didn't force me, but it's true that liquor dulls your inhibitions, I guess. At the time…" How could she explain that he'd seemed to need her so much that it hadn't seemed wrong?

"Paulie, I've asked myself a thousand times since then how I could have gone along with it." She shook her head. "I never come up with an answer I can accept."

Pauline got to her feet. Although her face was pale, her eyes were dry. "Thank you for being so honest," she said softly. "I guess you weren't the only one Carter manipulated, but it stops now, okay?"

Lily's vision blurred as relief overwhelmed her. "Okay."

The next morning when Lily carried three lattes into the house that she and Wade planned to remodel, he and Pauline were already standing in the empty living room. They'd all driven separately.

"I thought this called for something," she said, handing out the drinks. "To success." She lifted her cup in a toast.

"And successful partnerships," Wade added with a wink at Pauline.

"I was just telling Wade that I think this

is going to make a terrific office," Pauline said with a cheerful smile. Obviously, she had meant what she'd said in the garage about putting everything behind them.

At breakfast this morning when she had accepted Wade's invitation to check out the new acquisition, the knot that had been in Lily's chest for so long finally started to loosen. If only she could somehow mend the breach with Steve, as well, but she had no idea where to begin. Even though he'd kissed her, she doubted he was ready to forgive and forget.

"Earth to Lily," Wade said, waving his hand in front of her face. "Pauline wants to know if we're keeping the kitchen intact."

"Are you okay?" Pauline asked with a concerned frown.

"I'm fine." Lily tried to appear convincing. She could hardly admit in front of Steve's best friend that she hadn't been able to stop thinking about that kiss and what it meant. Although she still trusted Wade's discretion when it came to Jordan despite his meddling, she wasn't going to push her luck.

After taking another sip of coffee, Lily led the way through the dining room into the small kitchen. "I think this would make a good break room," she said as she looked around at the painted cabinets and outdated appliances. "If we take out the stove but leave the sink and the refrigerator, there would be room for a table and a microwave." She ran a hand over the old-fashioned linoleum counter. "What do you think?" she asked her sister.

"If this and the bathroom stay intact, do you have enough room for what you need?" Pauline asked.

Wade was about to reply when the front door opened. "Anyone home?" called out a familiar voice.

Lily's reaction was mixed. She hadn't known that Steve had been invited to come by, too, but she couldn't very well evade him forever.

"In the kitchen," Wade replied, cocking an eyebrow at Lily. "We're trying to decide where to start."

When Steve appeared in the doorway, she realized that she'd been holding her breath as she listened to his footsteps cross the hardwood floor. He wore a blue baseball cap, a faded but clean gray T-shirt, worn jeans and heavy work boots.

Even work clothes couldn't detract from his buff build or rugged male appeal.

"Good morning." His eyes widened slightly when he noticed Lily, but his grin didn't falter. "Great location," he added. "You were lucky to find a rezone in this neighborhood." Already he appeared to be evaluating the structure as he looked around.

"Want to see the rest of the place?" Wade offered. "We were about to show Pauline the bedrooms before she has to go back to work."

"Sure," Steve replied. "Lead on."

Lily remained silent as they toured the three bedrooms and the single bath. Steve's large form seemed to crowd each of the small rooms, but he didn't look at her again. She wondered if the other couple could feel the tension in the air as he and Wade studied the molding and thumped the walls.

"Great floors," Steve commented as they left the master bedroom. "All they'll need is refinishing. How are you going to allocate the space?"

"We've pretty much sorted that out," Lily volunteered, refusing to be intimidated by his presence any longer. Obviously the lip-lock they'd shared hadn't affected him. The least she could do to salvage her pride was to pretend the same.

"The living and dining rooms will be the reception and waiting areas that we'll share," she explained. "We'll each have an office and the third bedroom will be for storage since it's tiny. The bathroom will be remodeled and the tub removed. We're debating about the kitchen."

Steve nodded in apparent agreement. "It's all easily doable," he agreed. "More painting and cosmetic changes than structural, which will save time and money."

"That's what we figured," Wade replied. "Are you offering to help?"

Lily opened her mouth to protest, but Steve beat her to the punch.

"Sure thing," he said without glancing her way. "This morning I got an offer on the house that's nearly finished and the other one's ready for drywall." He smoothed a finger over his mustache. "And there's always the weekends."

The realization hit Lily that he must not be seeing anyone, at least not seriously. She tucked away the information to think about later when she was alone.

"This weekend we'll be helping Lily," Pauline volunteered cheerfully. "She and Jordan are moving."

Before Lily could speak, Steve turned the full power of his blue eyes on her. "Oh? Leaving home again?"

Ignoring his dig, she dragged up a casual smile. "A friend of a friend is spending a year abroad, so we're subletting his house on Jefferson, right near the high school." She jerked a thumb at Wade and Pauline, who stood with their shoulders touching. "Figured the love-birds could use some privacy."

"So you're no longer taking in boarders?" Steve asked Pauline. Before Lily had arrived, her sister had rented out some of the bedrooms in the big house.

Now she shook her head. "Dolly's the last one, but she knows that she's got a place with us for as long as she wants."

"Unless we decide to rent the apartment over the garage," Wade added, slinging his arm across her shoulder. "I fixed it up when she tossed me out of the main house."

Pauline blushed. "You know that wasn't my idea!" she exclaimed. "Blame Harriet Tuttle and her cronies."

Several of Pauline's best customers at the shop had made life difficult for her when they found out that Wade was living under her roof. She had been running for the city council at the time, but she'd lost to the owner of a big car dealership on the edge of town.

"Blame small-town attitudes," he retorted, leaning down to drop a kiss on her lips. "Most of the critics have come around, now that I've pledged to make an honest woman of her."

"And I do so appreciate it," Pauline replied in a squeaky falsetto with one hand over her heart.

"Man, this is getting too deep for me," Steve drawled. "You can probably thank Randy Wharton for giving everyone something new to talk about when he got arrested for leaving his house without his pants."

"I've heard that name before," Wade commented. "He must be the local drunk."

Lily remembered that Randy had been several years ahead of her in school, where he'd had a reputation as a clown. "I feel sorry for his family," she said softly.

Removing his cap, Steve raked a hand through his hair. "My wife and I went out with Randy and his wife a few times," he said. "Randy drank too much even then. Last I heard, when he got fired from the mill, Joyce took the kids and left."

Lily knew that Steve had been married for a few years. Even though his private life was none of her business, she wondered what had gone wrong and why he didn't have any kids. He'd certainly talked about wanting a family.

"As much as I'd like to hang out with the

rest of you, I've got to get back to work," Pauline announced. "Thanks for the latte, sis." She gave Steve a hug, patting his broad back. "Take care," she said.

Steve pressed a smacking kiss to her cheek. "Don't let your boyfriend find out about us," he teased, winking at the other man. "I hear he's the jealous type."

"You're no threat," Wade shot back. "Thanks for coming by."

Steve glanced at Lily. "Need a ride anywhere?"

His offer caught her by surprise. "No, th-thanks," she stammered, feeling like an idiot. "I've got my car."

"She has to stay here and help me," Wade said. "You can track her on your own time."

Steve laughed at his comment while Lily felt her face grow hot. "Later," he said as he headed out the door.

"We're not interested in each other," Lily protested after he'd gone. "That is so over."

As soon as the words had left her lips, she saw Wade and Pauline exchange a look that let Lily know she'd made a tactical error.

"Interesting," Wade murmured.

Pauline didn't reply, but her smile made Lily very, very uncomfortable.

Chapter Six

The morning sky was full of gray clouds, not that unusual for August on the Olympic Peninsula, when Steve stopped by his building site. Until the drywall was hung and taped, there wasn't much to do in his latest house. The one before it was nearly done and his next project was on hold until the building permit came through. His weekend rolled out before him as empty as Highway 19 at three in the morning.

On his way downtown, he'd told himself that Lily hadn't asked for his help today. Along with Wade and Pauline, she might have any number of hunky male volunteers lined up to move her.

The thought made Steve bare his teeth at his reflection in the rearview mirror as he waited in line at Jumpin' Java, a local espresso stand. Resolve wavering, he wandered up and down the aisles of the auto-parts store as he drank his coffee. After buying some car polish that he really didn't need, he convinced himself that checking out the activity at Pauline's old Victorian with its light blue paint and faded purple trim wasn't the same as giving in to temptation.

It stung his pride to find out that his attraction to Lily was as strong as ever despite the unceremonious way she had dumped him. He'd kidded himself into believing that he was over her, but then he remembered how she had melted against him for that timeless moment before pulling away. It shouldn't matter to him, but it did.

At Pauline's, the double garage doors were open and the trunk of Lily's car was up. Wade's truck was gone and Steve didn't see anyone around.

As he debated whether or not to stop, Jordan came out of the house with a cardboard box. When he saw Steve's truck, he hollered a greeting. Cover blown, Steve had no choice but to pull up on the grass next to Pauline's SUV.

"We're moving to our new house," Jordan announced after he'd stowed the box in Lily's half-full trunk and Steve had gotten out of his truck. "What are you doing here?"

Damn good question, Steve thought as he hitched up his jeans. "Thought I'd see if your mom needs another pair of hands," he replied. "Where is everyone?"

"Mom's packing up all the junk from her bathroom. Wade and Aunt Paulie took a load to the other house in his truck in case it starts to rain."

Just then, Lily came out to the porch with an armload of clothes on hangers. "Jordy, did you pack—" She stopped abruptly when she saw Steve.

"Morning," he said with an appreciative grin. "Don't you look cute."

Lily's cheeks turned pink and Jordan looked at her as though he'd never realized that his mom might be hot. Her hair was pulled into a ponytail that bobbed when she moved and she didn't appear to be wearing any makeup.

"I heard the truck, but I thought Wade was back," she said accusingly.

Steve took advantage of her momentary confusion to walk over and lift the clothes out of her arms. He had to resist the temptation to bury his nose in the fabric and breathe in her scent. "Where do you want these?" he asked instead.

"In the backseat." She scurried around him to open the car door. "It's nice of you to stop by," she said as he laid down the garments with care. "We don't have a lot of things to move, though, so everything's pretty much under control."

She turned to Jordan, who was watching them with his hands stuffed into the pockets of his baggy shorts. "Go get your DVDs from the family room."

"Duh!" he exclaimed, slapping his hand to his forehead. "I almost forgot."

"You can't have too much help when you move," Steve argued after the boy had left. "Now that I'm here—"

Lily's ponytail bobbed when she shook her head emphatically. "Thanks, but the sublease is furnished, so it's mostly just boxes."

The musical signal from the cell phone clipped to her waistband interrupted her. "It's Pauline," she said when she looked at the screen.

Steve leaned against the side of her car, feet

planted stubbornly and arms folded as he listened to the one-sided conversation.

"Oh, dear!" Lily exclaimed, turning her back on him. "How did it happen?"

Her words made him straighten abruptly. Hell, they must have gotten into an accident.

"Where are you now?" Lily asked after a pause. "Do you want me to come down? Are you sure?"

"Are they hurt?" he demanded.

She shook her head without looking up. "Yeah, I completely understand," she said. "No, don't worry about that. No, Steve's here and I'm sure we can use his truck."

He could hear Pauline's voice and she sounded upset. He hoped it wasn't serious. The two of them deserved a few breaks. Neither had had it easy.

"Yeah, I have the other key," Lily said. "It's not a problem, really. Call me when you know something more and tell him I'm really, really sorry." After another pause she said goodbye and ended the call while Steve waited impatiently.

"What happened?" he demanded. "Did someone hit them?"

"No," Lily replied with a sigh. "Poor Wade tripped and sprained his wrist when he was carrying the last box into the house. Now they're at the walk-in clinic, waiting to get it X-rayed. She has no idea how long it will take."

With Wade disabled, Lily had no choice but to accept Steve's offer to help. When his truck and her car were packed, he and Jordan followed her to a newer area of town where small houses in a mix of styles had been erected on the side of a hill facing the water.

"I've never been down this street before," Steve said after they'd parked. "You were lucky to find it, especially at this time of year."

It would be at least another month until the general end-of-summer exodus. "We were lucky to find anything," she retorted, "but I think this will suit Jordan and me just fine until I'm ready to buy something more permanent."

"So you're planning to stay awhile?" Steve asked as she unlocked the door and they carried things inside.

She wondered if he was really interested or just making conversation. "Crescent Cove is a good place to raise children," she replied as Jordan went down the hall to his new room. "I'm surprised you don't have any of your own."

A muscle jumped in Steve's cheek. "Oh,

but I do," he taunted softly. "Ask anyone around here."

Before she could think of a suitable reply, he set the carton of pots and pans in the kitchen where the cabinets had been painted a soft green to go with the checkered wallpaper.

"Steve, want to see my room?" Jordan called out eagerly. "There's a built-in desk and Mom's going to get me a new computer."

Lily couldn't very well blame Steve for his comment. He must have taken a lot of ribbing because of her and her son. She was lucky that he'd happened along today. Not wanting to take up more of his time, she crossed the living room on her way to the front door.

She could hear Jordan's chatter. He was the center of her life. After a rough start, he seemed to be dealing with all the changes in his young life. Although she could never actually wish death on anyone, part of her did feel enormous relief that she would never have to share him with a sleazeball like Carter Black.

Back in the driveway, she grabbed two stacked boxes from the tailgate of Steve's truck. They were heavier than she had expected and the top one began to slide when she tilted them.

"Whoa, there," he exclaimed from behind

her as he reached around to rescue the top box before it could fall to the concrete.

"Thanks," she said breathlessly. "They would have broken for sure."

"What's in here?" he asked as he followed her back to the house with a huge bag containing the bedding for her room.

"Turtles," she replied over her shoulder as she navigated the front step that had tripped Wade.

Apparently, Jordan was unpacking, because he hadn't come out of his room.

"Don't turtles need air holes?" Steve asked, following her.

She set her burden down on the dining room table. "They're not real. Some are glass or porcelain. Francis collected them." She had a sudden memory of the little creatures displayed all over his house. "His, um, family let me take them." Habit made her avoid saying *his partner*, even though she knew it hardly mattered now.

Steve dropped the bag onto the rug. "Did you love him a great deal?"

She met Steve's gaze, trying again without success to resist the tug of attraction. If her son hadn't been in the next room, she might have been tempted to find out how he would respond to a kiss that she initiated.

As though Steve could read her mind, his eyes darkened. "Lily?" His voice was slightly hoarse.

She stepped back, breaking the spell. "I loved Francis with all my heart," she declared, recognizing the irony of using her old friend as a shield after years of playing the same role for him.

Was that a flash of disappointment that crossed Steve's face or was she imagining things? Perhaps she owed him the truth. "Just not in the way people thought."

Immediately Steve's gaze sharpened. "What do you mean? Didn't he return your feelings?"

"We loved each other as friends," she explained, lowering her voice so Jordan wouldn't overhear. "Francis was gay, but he didn't want people to know."

It took Steve a few moments to process Lily's revelation about the man he'd assumed to have been her lover. A dozen questions leaped into his mind, but before he was able to voice even one, Wade's truck pulled into the driveway with Pauline behind the wheel.

"I'm so sorry!" Lily exclaimed as Wade got

out from the passenger side of the cab with his arm in a sling. "Are you okay?"

Wade lifted his bandaged wrist. "Had to be my right hand, of course, but I'll be fine."

"The doctor told him to use it as little as possible," Pauline added firmly. "No remodeling for at least two weeks."

Wade slung his free arm around Lily's shoulders and gave her a squeeze. The gesture irritated Steve for Pauline's sake, even though she didn't appear concerned.

"I'm the one who's sorry for letting you down," Wade told Lily, dropping his arm again. "You can't possibly get the work done on your own. Either we hire someone or we'll have to delay our grand opening."

Lily did a good job of covering up her disappointment, but Steve recalled how she used to fiddle with a strand of hair when she was upset. Right now she was twisting a lock that had worked its way loose of her ponytail, even while she smiled reassuringly.

"Don't worry about it," she told Wade. "I'm sure we can cancel the ads for it, even if we don't get back the deposits."

"Why didn't you get a cast on your arm?" Jordan interrupted from the front porch.

"It's not broken, just sprained," Wade replied. He and Pauline described the way he had tripped on a small rug that had gotten bunched in the doorway, landing awkwardly when he tried to catch his full weight on one arm.

Steve did some fast mental calculating while they talked. "Don't postpone your opening," he said when there was finally a break in conversation. "I'll help Lily with the work."

He was peripherally aware that they all looked at him, but the only face he saw was hers as he wondered if he had just made a huge mistake. Would he ever learn when it came to Lily?

Relief flashed across her face, only to be immediately doused. "Thank you so much for offering, but you can't possibly take that much time away from your own business," she said with a polite smile. "We've got a lot of work to do."

"I'm the boss and I know how to delegate," he replied firmly, mentally crossing his fingers and hoping he was right. "Besides, there's not much I can do until the subs finish with the painting and some other stuff." He grinned at Wade. "Sorry, buddy, but your timing couldn't have been better."

Wade shrugged. "Always glad to help."

Steve didn't think Wade's comment had

anything to do with remodeling. Ignoring his knowing smile, Steve turned back to Lily.

"What time do you want me to be there?"

"Where's the kid today?" Steve asked when he walked into the bedroom that was going to be Lily's office.

They had been working together for nearly a week now. Most days Wade was here at least part of the time, but today he was spending the day in Seattle with Pauline.

Lily looked up from the nail holes she was filling in the wall. "Jordan's at a friend's house." In hindsight, she almost wished she'd brought him with her, but Jeff had an above-ground pool. Much more fun than playing unwitting chaperone for your mother.

Steve gave her an exaggerated leer as he twirled one corner of his mustache. "So you and I are alone at last." So far he had proved to be a hardworking companion with a sense of humor that made her laugh despite her determination to keep her distance.

"You'd better watch yourself," she teased as she went back to work. "I could lose control and compromise your reputation."

When he didn't reply, she glanced over her shoulder, startled to find him closer than she had expected. As her eyes widened, he braced one hand on the wall next to her head and leaned down so she could feel his breath against her cheek.

"I'm willing to risk my reputation," he whispered. "How about you?"

Lily's survival instincts kicked in and she ducked under his arm. "I never flirt with the hired help," she quipped.

His killer grin didn't falter. "I volunteered for this gig," he drawled, "and technically, I'm not an employee. I'm in a class by myself."

"You certainly are," she murmured under her breath.

He must have heard her, because he chuckled. "Just so we're on the same page here."

To her immense relief, he walked past her to the doorway. "I'm going to unload the drywall so that I can enclose the kitchen wall and get it taped today," he said over his shoulder. "Be sure to sing out if you feel that control of yours starting to slip."

After he'd gone back outside, Lily collapsed against the wall and sucked in a deep breath. Steve might have been teasing, but he would never know how much she had wanted to close the last few inches separating them and press her mouth to his. She had to be losing her mind.

For the rest of the morning, she kept away from him as she patched picture holes in all three bedrooms. She and Wade had already decided that the single bathroom needed a makeover, since clients and staff would be sharing the facilities. Everything except the commode was going to be replaced and the tub was coming out. As she finally walked down the short hallway to the dining room, she was pleased with the progress they'd already made.

Steve had set up a saw in the driveway. Already the temperature was climbing and he'd removed his shirt. Mesmerized, Lily watched him through the living-room window as he worked. He'd shed his cap and a pencil stuck behind one ear poked through his hair. With every move he made, the muscles of his sculpted back and shoulders flexed beneath his deeply tanned skin. She wished he would turn so she could see his chest.

The hot bolt of desire that sizzled through her had nothing to do with memories of inexperienced teenage embraces and everything to do with an adult heat that made her feel as though she might burst into flames. Just as she realized how tightly she was gripping the putty knife in her hand, Steve turned his head.

His eyes met hers through the window. When he turned off the saw and came toward the house, nerves took over and she fled down the hall to the bathroom. Slamming the door shut behind her, she leaned against it and gulped in some air. Her heart thudded in her chest as she listened to the heavy tread of his work boots. With a shaking hand, she turned the flimsy lock, even as she wondered just what she was hiding from. She had no reason to fear him; it was herself she didn't trust.

"Lily!" he called through the door. "Are you okay? Is something wrong?"

She felt like an idiot for bolting. "I'm fine," she replied, licking suddenly dry lips. "I'll be out in a minute."

Pulse racing, she pressed her ear to the wooden panel. Was that his breathing she could hear or just a breeze stirring the tree branches?

"Okay, whatever," he said.

She waited for another few minutes after he departed before she opened the door a crack and peeked out. She could hear the whine of the saw.

Once again she wished she had brought

Jordan with her today. Steve never seemed to mind having an assistant who bombarded him with questions. He answered with a seemingly endless supply of patience as he kept Jordan busy. Without complaint, her son swept, he fetched tools from Steve's truck and the other day he'd helped tear out an old wall with a crowbar.

It was better for him to spend the day at a buddy's house, she told herself. He was developing a serious case of hero worship, but when the project was finished, her son was going to lose another father figure from his life.

Lily couldn't very well hide out in the only bathroom for the rest of the day. She stared at her reflection in the oval wall mirror that was due to be replaced. Too bad she hadn't grabbed her purse, she thought with grim humor. She could use a little lip gloss.

When she left the bathroom, she debated going outside, but she had no idea what to say. It was nearly lunchtime and she hadn't brought anything, so maybe she would offer to pick up hamburgers from the Shack. Wade had mentioned once that he'd gone there with Steve right after they met, so she knew he liked the food.

She was standing in the kitchen checking the cash in her purse when he walked in wearing his shirt again and carrying a length of drywall. He'd already framed the wall that would enclose the staff lounge.

When he saw her, he hesitated as though he expected her to freak again. "Everything okay?" he asked warily.

She could feel the blush working its way up her throat to her cheeks, one of the disadvantages of having fair skin. "Uh, yeah, thanks," she stammered.

He nodded as he leaned the panel against the far wall. "Good. I've got this all cut, so I can get it up before lunch."

She fidgeted with the birthstone ring that Francis had given her a few years before, telling her the blue topaz matched her eyes. The silence stretched between them awkwardly as Steve's gaze slid to her hand and back up to her face.

"I don't—" she began.

"Why don't we—" he said at the same time.

"You first," she told him, glad of the momentary respite.

To her surprise, he came over to stand in front of her. "I think I know what's wrong with us," he said, voice husky. Even if he hadn't been blocking her escape, she didn't think she'd be able to move. "We can't keep working together unless we get it resolved."

Deliberately, she folded her arms across her chest as she arched her eyebrows. "I have no idea what you're talking about."

"There's no reason for you to ever be nervous around me," he said, surprising her. "I hope you know that I'd never do anything to hurt you."

The idea that he might have the impression that she was afraid to be alone with him made her feel terrible. Automatically, she reached out to touch his bare forearm in order to reassure him.

"Please believe me when I say the idea never even occurred to me," she insisted. "I know you couldn't have changed that much."

His solemn expression relaxed into a grin. "Great. It's good to know that what I'm about to do won't send you screaming into the street scaring the neighbors."

Lily realized that he'd very neatly cornered her both literally and figuratively. She probably could have pushed past him, but at this moment in time, escape was the last thing she wanted. Instead she looked deep into his eyes. With a sigh of surrender, she gave in to the heat that had been building between them like a summer storm ever since he had kissed her behind the Crab Pot.

The intensity of his gaze on her mouth made her moisten her lips with the tip of her tongue.

"I'm lucky I haven't already cut off a couple of fingers, knowing you're in here," he said hoarsely. "Hell, I could have lost a hand and not even noticed."

"You keep talking and your break will be all used up," she murmured as growing need made her tremble.

Without warning, he clamped his hands around her waist and lifted her so that she was sitting on the counter. As she squeaked in alarm, he stepped between her knees and flattened his hands on the counter to frame her in. His eyes glittered and his expression radiated intensity.

"Kissing you again is all I've thought about for weeks," he growled. "Tell me you've thought about it, too."

As she took in the hunger etched into his face, Lily's defenses crumbled. "Every minute of every day," she admitted, locking her arms around his neck.

When he bent his head, she met him halfway and lost herself in the passion that exploded between them. For long, delirious moments, their lips and tongues dueled until every nerve in her body was on fire. Just as she figured she was destined to burn up like paper in a furnace, he pried his mouth from hers.

She dug her fingers into the front of his shirt, but he stepped away.

"I'm sorry," he said harshly, averting his face. "I thought I could do this, but I was fooling myself."

Chapter Seven

One more moment in Lily's arms and Steve would have laid her down on the counter and climbed on top of her. His control hadn't been this shaky since he was a teenage punk on hormone overload.

What must Lily think of him—the poor sap who hadn't managed to get over her? He dragged in a deep breath and let it out slowly, willing his legs to hold him up and his brain to clear of its red haze. Gradually, as control seeped back, he realized that she hadn't moved. Expecting to see pity or even distaste stamped on her lovely face, he finally lifted his head.

The vow that it wouldn't happen again froze

on his tongue as she finally turned away from him and slid down from the counter where he'd set her. She wasn't quick enough, though, to hide the tears swimming in her eyes. Without thinking, he snagged her wrist to keep her from leaving.

"Oh God, Lil, did I scare you? Hurt you?" The possibility made his heart stutter in his chest. "I never meant—"

"Please just let me go." Her face was averted, her voice flat, making him feel like the all-time prize jerk of the century.

"Look at me," he pleaded, barely resisting the urge to take her into his arms and make things even worse. He'd never forced himself on a woman. What the hell had he been thinking? "Tell me you forgive me."

"Of course," she murmured. "You can't help it that you don't find me…attractive."

Of all the accusations he expected her to make, that wouldn't have been in the top ten thousand. It startled a rueful laugh out of him before he could prevent it.

"Are you crazy!" Without thinking, he laid his hand on her shoulder. She stiffened, but he'd be damned if he would allow her to think for one more second that he didn't find her desirable—so much so that he was in danger of losing his mind.

The hell with his pride; it was Lily who mattered. "Baby, do you think that's a gym sock stuffed down the front of my jeans?"

What an elegant way to put it, Lindstrom. First you assault her and then you gross her out. Before he could apologize yet again, she gazed up at him with a bemused expression.

"Are you just trying to spare my feelings?" she asked, a frown forming between her delicate brows.

He would have jumped off a bluff without a chute if it wiped away the uncertainty he saw in her eyes. Instead, he took her hand and placed it firmly on the front of his fly. The slight pressure made sweat pop out on his forehead.

"You tell me," he said, voice raw.

He expected her to pull away. When he felt her fingers trace his throbbing length through the denim, every cell in his body leaped to attention and his knees, already shaky, threatened to buckle. He braced one hand against the counter, muscles quivering. Served him right if she was only teasing to pay him back.

"You really want to test me like that?" he ground out through clenched teeth. So much for regaining control, or the idea that he scared her. It would have been funny if he was capable of laughter at the moment.

Instead the only sound in the room was his own harsh breathing.

"My goodness," she whispered, sliding her fingers down to cup him lightly, "is that because of me?"

Without a drop of blood left in his brain, Steve feared he might black out. "It's sure as hell not from the paint fumes," he croaked. "Are you getting even with me?"

She stepped closer, nearly breaking his heart when she moved her hand back up to his waist. "What do you think?"

"That I'm dreaming or I died in my sleep, but either way works for me."

To his dismay, she removed her hand. "This isn't getting the remodeling done," she said in a voice that sounded amazingly normal.

"What?" Hunger still sizzled through him as she brushed at her lashes with her fingertips to remove the trace of tears. "You expect me to run power tools after this?" he demanded.

Her smile nearly blinded him with its brightness. "It's all in your ability to concentrate, big boy. I'm sure you'll do just fine."

She was suddenly altogether too damned

cheerful and he had no idea how to interpret his new nickname. Being a guy, he hoped it was a compliment.

"Wait, wait, wait," he insisted as she left him standing alone in the kitchen, her hips swaying enticingly. "This won't do at all."

Immediately she swung back around. "You said the same thing after you kissed me," she reminded him. "Do you even know what you want?"

He ran a hand over his face, wishing he'd stayed outside, minding his own business. The power saw was far less dangerous than the blonde standing in front of him, blue eyes shooting sparks.

Folding his arms across his chest, he leaned against the counter. "You're driving me crazy," he said bluntly.

Lily tried to read the meaning behind his belligerent expression without success. "Define *crazy*," she demanded.

She felt as though she had just taken a ride on an emotional roller coaster and her patience, never her strongest characteristic, was beginning to shred.

A car drove by, stereo blasting. She nearly jumped out of her skin as she realized that anyone could walk in off the street. A moment ago she had been tempted to strip off her clothes and beg Steve to take her.

"Let's see if you can understand this." Steve hauled her back into his arms. His mouth was hot and urgent on hers, his tongue demanding entrance. Once again, she was plunged down a steep slope, stomach dropping away, unable to breathe as she clung to his muscular arms and gave herself up to the undeniable force between them.

He released her so abruptly that she staggered before catching herself.

"Still think we can work together as if there's nothing more going on between us?" he taunted. "Or are you starting to get how badly I want you?"

The blatant reminder of her hand on his crotch made her cheeks flame. Just because a man got physically aroused didn't prove anything, though. Steve had plenty of motive for wanting to humiliate her after the way she'd treated him in the past.

"Just what is it that you're suggesting we do about it?" she asked carefully.

His casual shrug drew her attention to his powerful build. The image of him standing shirtless in the driveway was enough to make her light-headed. As a teenager, he had been strikingly attractive, but the man he'd become ignited her senses on a level she wouldn't have believed possible.

"We're adults, not kids living some fantasy." He studied her through narrowed eyes. "Let's follow this attraction between us to its obvious conclusion so we can move on."

The idea of sharing that final intimacy with him almost took her breath away, but his breezy dismissal of the young love they had shared stung like a slap in the face. She hadn't left because she no longer loved him, but neither was he still the boy she had known.

"You're saying that I should fall into bed with you because you've got an *itch*?" She infused her tone with disbelief. Was it a quickie he was after, a fling? "Have you forgotten that I have a child to consider, one who happens to think you walk on water?"

"I wasn't suggesting that we tell him!" Steve exclaimed. "We're clever enough to keep it private."

She shook her head, stunned that she wasn't totally repelled by the idea of sneaking around in order to have sex with him. "Let's just forget any of this ever happened," she said firmly, ignoring the ribbons of desire still curling inside her. Had she no pride? "I need to get the walls prepped so I can start painting tomorrow."

"Just think about it," he called after her as she went back down the hall. "We should just get it over with and clear the air. The idea makes sense."

To a guy, perhaps. "Like that's going to happen anytime soon," she muttered beneath her breath. He'd made it perfectly clear that he had no interest in getting reacquainted with her as a person, nor was he willing to talk about himself or his divorce. The smartest thing she could do would be to keep her distance until Wade was able to come back.

He had blown it big time today, Steve told himself ruefully as he studied the dividing wall he'd constructed between the dining room and kitchen. In place of the previous open access, he would add a door that could be closed to give the staff some privacy. Tomorrow after he met with the finish plumber, who was ready to set the fixtures at his "other" house, he would see if Wade wanted him to start on the bathroom here.

He was beginning to feel like a juggler as he lugged his toolbox out to his truck, checked around one last time and locked the front door behind him. Lily had practically sneaked from the house a little while before, calling out a goodbye as she blew through the living room and he was on his knees in the kitchen.

Just call him *Mr. Romance* with his ham-fisted suggestion that they hook up and burn off some energy. What had he expected, that she would invite him to adjourn to a cheap motel out on the highway?

All that blood draining from his head must have affected his mind because it sure as hell didn't seem to be functioning at a human level today. After he slapped the steering wheel strong enough to make his hand sting, he pulled out of the driveway. The sudden blare of a horn almost made him leap from his seat. As he slammed on his brakes, a red convertible swerved around him, burning rubber as it sped away.

Steve let out a string of curses he seldom used. One way or another, he'd better get his life under control before he did something to royally screw it up.

Lily thought seriously about taking the next day off after she'd spent a restless night trying not to think about Steve's outrageous suggestion or the fact that Jordan wasn't asleep down the hall.

He had been invited to stay at his friend's house and go to the Woodland Park Zoo in Seattle today. Lily had visited the zoo many times as a child, but she'd heard that enlightened attitudes and extensive upgrades had changed it significantly. Someday soon, she hoped to take him there herself.

She had finished unpacking most of their belongings and she'd added some personal touches to the furnished house. The rest of their things were stacked in the attached garage next to the owner's silver Beemer. She was supposed to meet Wade at the paint store this morning, so she couldn't very well play hooky just because she'd come down with a bad case of lust.

She peeled off her nightshirt and stepped into the spacious shower. Twenty minutes later, she stowed her notes and color chips, a sack lunch and two water bottles into her car. She locked the front door and drove to the paint store.

Wade was standing out front when she arrived, his arm in a sling. His expression brightened when he saw her.

"I hope you haven't been waiting long,"

she said as he held open her door with his good hand.

"Just got here," he replied.

She was about to ask how he was able to drive when she noticed Steve walking toward them from the outdoor furniture store next door.

"Morning, Lily." He touched his fingers to the brim of his cap in a parody of politeness. His cocky grin and sweeping gaze made her tingle all over. "You look ravishing, as usual."

She'd dressed in a pair of frayed cutoffs, a knit shirt and tennis shoes that were already paint-spattered. Her only makeup was lip gloss and her hair was anchored with a clip that left the ends sticking up like saw grass. Steve, however, managed to look deliciously masculine as usual in snug jeans, a T-shirt that hugged his muscular chest and work boots. All he needed was a hard hat to complete the picture.

"I could have picked you up," she told Wade accusingly, even though finding room for the five-gallon paint cans in her car might have been a challenge.

With a patently innocent expression, he shrugged. "Steve offered."

As she led the way into the store, she could

have sworn that he turned a chuckle into a cough behind her back. If the two of them wanted to act like a couple of juveniles, she wasn't going to react.

There was a display of wallpaper samples on one side of the store. On the opposite wall were sections containing brushes, painters' tape, applicators of every description, rollers and pans, spray guns and various other tools. In the back corner were ladders of different heights and scaffolding.

The same gray-haired clerk who'd been working the last time she came in was waiting on two older women she didn't recognize. "Welcome back," he called out to Lily before he greeted Wade and Steve. "I'll be with you folks in a few minutes."

"That's fine," she replied as she walked over to the paint recommended by a consumer site she had researched on the computer.

Once she and Wade had agreed on coordinating shades of cream, taupe and soft green for the interior walls, they added brushes, rollers and other supplies to the growing order. The brick exterior would be pressure-washed, the shutters and trim painted glossy black. The new front door they had ordered from a Native American woodcarver and the brass hardware would be ready before the grand opening.

"I brought some drop cloths we can use on the floor," Steve said when they were done. He used his contractor's license to get them a discount while Lily double-checked her list to make sure they hadn't forgotten anything.

"I think I'll go on over to the house," she said brightly.

Even though Steve had stayed out of the discussion about paint colors, she'd wondered what he thought of her suggestions. A break from the awareness humming through her like a low-grade electrical charge would be welcome.

"I'll be right back," the clerk said. "I need to check on one of the tints and make sure I have it in stock."

"I'll see you in a while." Waggling her fingers in a casual wave, Lily made her escape.

Steve couldn't resist watching her long, bare legs beneath the fringe of her cutoffs as she walked out to her car. The prospect of spending another day around her was both punishment and reward. Last night, he'd sat on his deck with the dogs for a long time, watching the stars come out and wondering whether he had lost his mind.

"Don't trip on your tongue," Wade said dryly, startling him.

"I like looking at beautiful women," Steve replied defensively, folding his arms across his chest. "So sue me."

"You like looking at my fiancée's sister," Wade argued. "It's as obvious as elk turds in the snow, so you might as well admit it."

"The only thing that's obvious is that she's pretty," Steve said through clenched teeth.

Wade gave a snort of disbelief as the clerk came back to the register. Lucky for Wade, punching a smart-ass with one arm in a sling in front of a witness wasn't Steve's style.

The clerk handed over the paperwork for his signature. "It will take a while to mix the paint," he said. "Is this your cell number? I can call you when it's ready."

"That works." Steve scrawled his name at the bottom of the page. "Thanks."

Pushing open the door with his shoulder, Wade led the way outside. "Glad that's done." He jiggled his arm in its sling. "Maybe I could learn to paint left-handed."

"Why did Lily have to get even better looking than before?" Steve grumbled, unable to stop himself as they reached his truck.

Wade clapped him on the back with his

good hand. "Because the Mayfield women were put on this earth to torment us poor, clueless males until we howl for mercy."

Steve remembered the rough patch Pauline and his buddy had gone through, even breaking up for a short time before Wade worked up the stones to propose. Although Steve couldn't be happier that it had all worked out for his friend, he had no intention of putting himself through that kind of torture.

"Speak for yourself, old man," he taunted as he climbed into his truck and fastened his seat belt. "I'm not dumb enough to stick my finger into that particular light socket again." Just because he experienced a surge of raw lust every time he thought about Lily didn't mean he planned to let her tie his feelings into great big knots again, too.

"Trust me," Wade drawled as they left the parking lot, "your turn will come. Then you'll find out that it's not your finger you need to watch out for, my friend. We like to think we're in control, but that's just a male fantasy. It's right up there with the one about being stalked by a supermodel."

Steve turned the corner and drove past City Hall, a historical brick building dripping with elaborate terra-cotta trim that had been restored a few years before. Next to it was the new safety building that housed the police and fire departments. In the parking lot on the side were several police cruisers.

"Pauline may have spun your head around backward, but when I got married, I knew exactly what I was doing." Steve thumped his chest with his fist for emphasis.

"I'm sure you're right," Wade agreed easily. "Remind me again how that marriage is working for you."

"Very funny." Steve whipped the truck into the driveway in front of Wade's future office. "Just because I wouldn't mind doing the horizontal polka with Lily doesn't mean I plan on getting in over my head, that's all."

"We never do," Wade said, slipping in the last word like a shiv between Steve's ribs.

"I'm glad you were able to come with me today," Pauline said happily as she drove down Highway 3 toward the Silverdale Mall.

"I wouldn't have missed it," Lily replied. "Thanks for inviting me." She glanced at her sister's profile, grateful that the two of them had managed to find their way past everything that had kept them apart for so long. Before Lily's return from LA, she would never have believed that just a few weeks later she would be going to Nordstrom with Pauline to look at wedding dresses.

"What's Wade going to wear for the ceremony?" Lily asked. "A tux?"

Changing lanes to allow a car to shoot past them, Pauline shook her head. "A dark suit, I think. He was going to talk to Steve and then see if you'd mind them taking Jordan shopping with them."

"Yes, Wade mentioned it already. It's no surprise that my son's attitude toward the idea of going clothes shopping did an immediate one-eighty when I told him."

Yesterday, when Steve had shown up with the paint and no Wade, she'd stayed busy in her office, covering the walls with the soft green she'd chosen. Halfway through the afternoon, she'd heard his cell ring and then he poked his head in through the doorway to tell her that he had to leave.

"I'll lock the door after me," he'd said. "Will you be okay here until I get back?"

She'd felt a reluctant tug of appreciation for his concern, even as she assured him that she would be just fine alone. By the time she was done and had washed everything out, it was after five and he hadn't come back yet. She had spent the evening listening to Jordan's description of the zoo and this morning she had left him with Wade.

As soon as things calmed down, she promised herself silently, she would take her son somewhere fun, just the two of them. Maybe they would spend the night in Victoria or go exploring along the Seattle waterfront. He would love the aquarium and the Pike Place Market.

"I hope I can find something I like," Pauline murmured.

"What type of outfit are you going to look for?" Lily asked her. "Tailored or feminine?"

Pauline chuckled. "That would be what you'd expect from me, right? Perhaps it's time to break out of the mold. I want to find something that will knock Wade's eyes out."

"Good for you," Lily exclaimed. "I'm sure Nordstrom will have exactly what you're looking for."

"Now, I don't want you to argue with me," Pauline said, reverting to the big-sisterly tone she'd always used whenever she'd wanted her own way, "but I'm paying for your outfit, too. Dress, shoes, bag and whatever. My treat."

Lily had intended to buy Pauline's dress as a wedding present. Normally, she would have argued, but this time she held her tongue. "Thank you," she said as graciously as she could manage. "That's very sweet of you."

Pauline's smile was reward enough for letting her have her way. "You'll be the loveliest attendant this town has ever seen," she said. "I almost wish we were having a bigger wedding, just so more people would get a look at you."

Her comment moved Lily deeply. "Are you nuts?" she demanded in order to prevent herself from getting weepy. "I thought a small ceremony was a nonnegotiable part of Wade's proposal."

"Brat," Pauline retorted. "You're right, though. Neither of us wanted anything elaborate. It's not about that—it's about making a commitment to share our lives."

Seeing her sister's happy glow, Lily felt a twinge of envy. Would she ever find someone like that, or had she thrown away her only chance for true love, just like a spoiled child would toss aside a toy?

Chapter Eight

"Did you find a dress?" Wade asked as he walked into the kitchen at Pauline's house.

Lily watched her sister get up from the table where the two of them had been enjoying a glass of iced tea after their forty-mile drive up from Silverdale, which was across the Hood Canal Floating Bridge. Pauline slipped into her fiancé's arms like a homing pigeon come to roost.

"We both found outfits for the nuptials," she replied after she had greeted him with a kiss. "You know you can't see mine until the wedding, though."

When Wade's lean features softened into

a smile brimming with affection, Lily felt a surge of envy fill the region around her heart.

With a teasing expression, Pauline leaned back in the crook of his arm. "I found a little something for the honeymoon, too."

His eyes narrowed and Lily suspected they had both forgotten that anyone else was in the room. "You don't need clothes for that," he murmured.

"Minor on board, so cut it out, you two." Steve appeared in the laundry room doorway carrying two big pizza boxes. Jordan followed him into the kitchen.

"What does that mean?" he asked, looking up at his new idol.

"It means no mushy stuff." Wade released Pauline and she patted his cheek before backing away. The ring on her finger, a platinum knot set with diamonds, sparkled in the light. Her cheeks were flushed a becoming shade of pink. It was good to see her so happy.

Lily could smell the enticing aroma from the boxes Steve set on the counter. When his gaze met hers, she scooted back her chair, fighting the insistent tug of attraction.

"Jordan and I have got to be going," she announced to no one in particular.

"Mom, we brought pizza," he protested. "Can't we stay and eat?"

She was about to refuse when Wade chimed in. "We'll never be able to finish it without you two to help." He ruffled Jordan's hair. "The kid here can probably eat one all by himself."

Tossing up her hands in defeat, Lily sank back down. "I'm outnumbered," she grumbled. The instant she realized how ungrateful she must sound, she forced a smile. "Thanks, Wade. That's awfully nice of you."

"Steve is the one you should thank," he replied cheerfully. "Bringing pizza was his idea."

Steve removed his cap and pushed a hand through his hair. Now that she was used to the longer style—and the mustache—she thought the look suited him.

"Ham and pineapple was always your favorite," he said, deliberately reminding her of their shared past. "I hope it still is."

Lily nodded and then looked away. Going to Bella's Italian Restaurant with the gang after a football game had always been a special treat. The girls would still be dressed in their cheerleader outfits and the guys wore their letterman jackets. It almost made up for all the hours Steve spent at team practices, leaving her to brood over being left alone.

Looking back, she realized how immature her attitude had been, and how vulnerable she'd been to Carter's attention.

Appetite gone, she wished she could leave, but there was Jordan to consider. Clearly he enjoyed being a part of the group.

Pauline opened the refrigerator door and peered inside. "Who wants soda and who wants beer?"

"I'll take a brewski," Jordan replied in a deep voice.

The others all laughed as Wade clamped a hand onto his shoulder. "You'll have to stick with soda for a few more years, sport."

"At least another twenty, if I have my wish," Lily muttered. "I'll take diet if you have it, sis."

In just a couple of minutes, they were all seated at the long dining room table with plates of pizza in front of them.

"Did you ladies have a good time today?" Wade asked before taking a large bite of his slice.

Pauline winked at Lily, who felt her spirits lift. "I'd say the trip was a success," Pauline replied. "Spending money is always fun."

Lily couldn't help but return her smile. For the longest time, Lily had missed her sister more than she had thought possible.

"Thank you again for buying my bridesmaid's outfit," Lily said before she began to nibble on a slice of Hawaiian pizza, which was still her favorite.

"I'm delighted with your choice," Pauline replied. "You look absolutely ravishing in it."

Steve looked at Lily. "Define *ravishing*."

She knew she'd turned bright red. "You'll have to wait," she said sweetly.

She loved the dress they'd found for her at a small boutique. It was short, like Pauline's, with a strapless bodice and a layered handkerchief hemline. Unlike Pauline's, which was made of textured cream silk trimmed with delicate matching lace and tiny ribbon roses, Lily's had been hand-painted in watercolor swirls of light blue and aqua. Her high-heeled leather sandals were also blue.

"Mom!" Jordan's voice penetrated Lily's thoughts. Judging from his impatient expression, it wasn't the first time he'd addressed her.

"What is it, honey?" she asked, aware that everyone was watching her.

"Is Steve going to be your date at the wedding?" Jordan asked.

"What gave you that idea?" She winced inwardly at her own defensive tone, careful not to look at the man in question. "He and I will be part of the ceremony, but you'll be my escort."

Her son's eyes widened with alarm. "Me? What will I have to do?"

"You're going to help me to keep the old man here from passing out from prewedding jitters," Steve drawled, earning a chuckle from Pauline.

"Pre-what?" Jordan demanded.

"That's what *other* guys come down with before reciting their vows," Wade replied smoothly, "but not me. Marrying your aunt is the smartest thing I'll ever do."

"That's so sweet," Pauline murmured while Steve stuck his finger in his mouth in a gagging motion. He and Jordan exchanged high fives.

"It's kinda sad," Steve teased, "to see a guy who's so far gone."

"I think it's kind of refreshing," Lily blurted.

Steve's brows rose up like twin arches as he studied her thoughtfully.

"What?" she finally asked.

He shook his head, but he wore a mysterious smile. "Oh, nothing."

Vowing to ignore him, she concentrated on her pizza while Pauline and Wade reviewed their wedding plans.

"I've got the cross-stitched inserts nearly finished for the invitations," she said. "Thank goodness the guest list is a short one."

"I second that," Wade said gravely. "Too bad my folks can't make it, though." He didn't sound the least bit sorry. "Mom doesn't feel up to making the trip from Florida."

Lily couldn't imagine missing her son's wedding.

"We'll have to visit them later," Pauline replied tactfully. She had mentioned to Lily that he wasn't close to his parents. Apparently, they hadn't supported him when he was briefly implicated in his business partner's embezzlement of client funds back in San Francisco. It had all been sorted out eventually and his partner sent to prison, but not before Wade's professional reputation had been ruined.

"Can I have another piece of combo supreme?" Jordan asked Lily.

"If you're still hungry." She was relieved that his appetite had shown such a dramatic improvement. After Francis died and she had brought Jordan up from LA, he'd lost interest in food for a while.

"I can hardly wait for you to open your accounting business," Pauline said to her. "My old tax adviser has been threatening to retire."

"I'll give you a good rate," Lily replied. "You'll be my first client."

"Please don't talk about income tax," Steve muttered. "It gives me a headache."

"Who does yours?" Pauline asked.

He darted a glance at Lily. "Last year I used someone in Poulsbo."

"And this year?" Pauline persisted.

He shrugged and looked away. "I, uh, missed the deadline."

"My goodness, that was over three months ago," Lily exclaimed without thinking. "Did you file an extension?"

He twisted the corner of his mustache as he stared at his plate. "I don't think so."

She rolled her eyes. "Sounds like you need some help."

Immediately he sat up straighter. "Are you offering? My state revenue taxes are overdue, too."

She felt cornered, but she could hardly refuse at this point, especially after he'd put in so many hours helping to remodel the office.

"I suppose you keep your receipts in a shoe box," she guessed.

He grinned sheepishly. "Just the ones I can find."

Even if he had already filed his taxes for the year, Steve would have been happy to file them again and pay double if it meant spending more one-on-one time with Lily. He had enough experience under his belt to avoid getting sucked into a situation with *heartache* stamped all over it. He was pretty sure, though, that what happened in the past hadn't really been about him. It was an act of rebellion by an immature teen in pursuit of a dream.

"You've had women over to dinner before and it's no big deal," he muttered aloud as he paced nervously between the entryway and the kitchen. Both dogs watched him from the living-room floor and he swore he could read concern in their dark eyes. Or perhaps it was the steaks marinating on a plate in the kitchen that had captured their interest.

The next time he'd seen Lily, a few days after the informal pizza feed, she had started in on him. Jeez, was he the first person to ever miss the deadline on his income tax?

"I meant to make an appointment, but I

kept forgetting," he had admitted, just to shut her up. "Then I figured that I was going to be late, anyway, so I'd just pay the fines and get caught up next year. It's no big deal."

"No big deal!" she'd squeaked, staring at him as though he'd just confessed to strangling his grandmother. "You need to file as soon as possible." She had even waved a scolding finger under his nose, which made him chuckle.

Which had obviously annoyed her even more, because she stamped her foot. Lordy, but she was cute when she was annoyed. Her cheeks turned pink, her eyes practically shot blue sparks and her lips were all puckered up in a sexy little pout. All could think about was scooping her up and kissing her senseless.

From there, it had been almost too easy to persuade her to come over and help him with those pesky taxes, especially when he'd promised to throw in dinner. Or perhaps the reason she hadn't offered much of an argument was because she'd been mulling over his earlier suggestion that they work off the sexual tension between them in bed. He hadn't given up on that yet.

He stood in front of the refrigerator with the door open until the cool air snapped him back to reality. The only reason that Lily was coming over tonight was because she had a good heart. She didn't want to see him dragged off to the federal pen in handcuffs and shackles.

Would they actually do that? he wondered as he programmed music into the built-in speaker system in the family room. He was barely finished when the front door chimed. Both dogs followed him down the hall to see who was here.

"Sit," Steve told them firmly. With his hand on the brass knob, he waited for them to obey and then he opened the door.

"Hi," Lily said. She was dressed casually in a blue striped blouse and jeans. Her hair hung loose, reminding him of how it felt to run his fingers through it. As always, her delicate beauty was like a blow to his solar plexus, catching him off guard and taking his breath.

"Thanks for coming," he said as he opened the door wider and spotted her briefcase. Unless she carried her props and a party hat inside, she really did intend to help with his taxes.

"No problem." She appeared more relaxed than he felt. "This is a beautiful place. I'm impressed."

"Thank you." When he inclined his head,

the faint scent of flowers filled his nostrils. He was tempted to bury his face in her hair, but he resisted. "Come on in."

"Ooh, how cute!" She extended her free hand toward the dogs, whose tails thumped in unison against the tiled floor. "My son told me about you two."

Immediately they rose to check her out while she tried to rub their heads.

"Which is Sonic and which is Seahawk?" she asked. After Steve made introductions, she called each one by name amid more caresses.

Steve had no doubt that man's best friends would abandon him without a glance if she asked. "Would you like some wine?" he offered over his shoulder as he led the way to the dining room. Perhaps liquid fortification would make the task ahead slightly less intimidating.

"Water or iced tea would be nice," she said politely as she followed him past the dining-room table, set with two places. At the far end a couple of shoe boxes full of papers were stacked.

"You weren't kidding, were you?" she asked, setting down her briefcase.

He filled crystal tumblers with ice. "'Fraid

not." By the time he'd poured their tea and added a lemon wedge to each glass, she had laid out a legal pad, some pencils with points that would put out a man's eye and several folders.

There was no party hat in sight. Hopes dwindling, he slid open the patio door. "Why don't you come outside while I cook the steaks?" he suggested.

Lily went straight to the railing. "What a wonderful view," she exclaimed. "Is that Everett across the water?"

"Whidbey Island," he replied. "It's the longest island in the country." As soon as the words left his mouth, he felt like a tour guide. "Uh, I read that somewhere."

She smiled brightly. "I envy you. A water view is so restful."

He mulled over her comment while the steaks sizzled, trying without success to analyze it for hidden meaning. When the meat was done, he put the dogs into their run and carried the platter back inside while Lily followed with their glasses.

"Have you lived here long?" she asked.

"About four years," he replied, holding out her chair. "I like to watch the ships go by." He set the salad bowl and dressing bottles on the table. "Help yourself while I get the rest."

He split the baked potatoes that had been in the oven, put them on plates with the meat and grabbed the little rack with the bowls of toppings. After he'd refilled their glasses, he joined her at the table.

Her presence in the house he had built wasn't something he'd ever visualized, but the sight of her affected him more strongly than he had expected.

"Jordan wants a dog, but the lease I signed doesn't allow for a pet," she said as she buttered her potato.

"Did he have one in California?" Steve asked. He wondered if they had lived in one of the fancy houses he had seen on television.

"Francis was terribly allergic," she replied after she'd eaten a bite of salad. "There were saltwater aquariums scattered throughout the house, but nothing with fur."

Francis again. If Lily was telling the truth and he wasn't Jordan's father, then who was? Steve hated to think her first time had been with some guy she barely knew, not after she and Steve had decided to wait. Given their feelings for each other and their raging hormones, waiting hadn't been easy.

When he laid down his knife and fork,

steak only half eaten, she gave him a puzzled glance. "Not hungry?"

"I guess facing my tax return has taken away my appetite," he replied. "The dogs will finish for me."

"Trust me," she said with a grin, "it won't be too painful. This meal is far too good to waste."

Since she was watching him expectantly, he picked up his fork again. "I'm glad you think so." He didn't need to know her life history in order to sleep with her, he reminded himself. Despite all signs to the contrary, she couldn't possibly be the sweet, wonderful girl he'd fallen in love with. As long as he remembered that, he'd be fine.

A little while later when they were done eating, Lily scooted back her chair and carried her dishes to the kitchen.

"That was delicious," she said as she whisked away his empty plate. "I'll help with the cleanup so we can get started."

"Leave it," he said with a dismissive wave. "I'll do it later."

He had been enjoying their desultory conversation, mostly about the people they'd both known and all the changes to the surrounding area. As if by silent agreement, they had avoided anything more personal, but he wasn't ready to abandon the pretense of getting to know a beautiful woman with whom he shared no baggage.

"What, no small talk before the main event?" he teased as he got to his feet. "No foreplay?"

Her cheeks turned slightly pink and her gaze refused to meet his, both of which he considered encouraging signs.

"Let's get down to business," she said briskly, scooting her chair closer to the table. She handed him a form. "I'd like you to fill this out while I look through your boxes."

For the next hour, they made steady progress as he answered questions and helped her to separate the mound of paperwork. She obviously had a real knack for the career she had chosen, making him wonder if she had any regrets about not becoming a star.

"I'm impressed," he exclaimed when everything was sorted. "Who knew that under that gorgeous exterior lurks a sharp intelligence and a head for numbers?"

He'd only been kidding, but as soon as the words were out and he saw her expression freeze up, he knew he'd made a grave tactical error. Her face was devoid of feeling, her eyes as blank as a blue wall when her gaze met his.

"Thank you. Now, if you'll excuse me, I'll pack this all up and get going." The temperature in the room had plunged to somewhere below zero as she slid back her chair and stood up.

Steve got to his feet so quickly that his chair fell over behind him, but he barely noticed as he wrapped his fingers around her bare wrist. He was a little surprised that her skin was still warm to the touch.

"Come on, Lil, you know I was only kidding. I *always* knew how smart you were." When she tried to tug her arm free, he tightened his fingers. "Wasn't I the one who always said you were more than a pretty face?" he demanded. "Maybe I was just a football player, but I knew from the first time we talked that you had more going for you than looks."

She'd stopped struggling, but she kept her face turned away from him. "Let me go."

He couldn't stop himself from giving her a little shake. "Not until you look at me," he replied grimly. This sure as hell wasn't the way he'd intended the evening to end.

When she finally lifted her head, he expected to see spitting temper on her face.

When he noticed that her eyes were moist, his heart kicked over in his chest.

"Aw, honey, I'm sorry," he said. "It was a dumb thing for me to say."

"That's true." A little of the spunk he'd come to expect of her crept back into her voice. "How'd you like to be called a dumb jock because you were good at sports?"

He slid his arms around her. "I've been called that more than once. Now, if I tell you that I know for a fact that you're not only extremely smart, breathtakingly gorgeous, but also very, very talented, will you forgive me?"

For an endless moment, she looked up at him as he stood motionless, afraid to move and break the spell he could feel spinning out around them.

Suddenly one of the dogs barked sharply from the outside run. It had probably spotted a bird or a stray cat on the deck.

Lily jerked in Steve's embrace. "Thank you," she murmured. "I'll let you know if I have questions about your taxes."

He tightened his arms. "No, you can't leave."

She tipped back her head, managing to look down her nose even though he topped her by half a foot. "Oh?"

"Not until I know things are okay between us," he improvised quickly.

When she drew in a breath, he could feel her breasts press against him. His reaction was as swift as it was predictable, firing up the need that had been simmering within him all evening.

A need she couldn't fail to notice as she stood in the circle of his arms.

"Yes, everything's fine," she said dutifully. "Now I should go."

"It's still early," he argued. "Why not stay for a while and tell me how you feel about my earlier suggestion." He slid his hands down her back to her waist. It felt as narrow as it had back in school.

"What suggestion would that be?" A tremor in her voice spoiled her facade of mild curiosity.

If she had tried to push him away, Steve would have released her instantly. When he leaned closer and she didn't protest, he was shocked that he didn't spontaneously combust from the heat they generated. If she was toying with him to see how far he would go before she shut him down, he would sink to his knees and bawl like a baby.

"Where's your son tonight?" he suddenly thought to ask.

His question must have caught her off guard. "Uh, at a friend's," she stammered. "Why?"

"When are you supposed to pick him up?" Steve would have given half his assets for another hour with her, two if she was willing.

She sighed, making his heart stutter as he felt the slight yielding of her body. "Not until tomorrow morning."

Lily had sworn to herself that she wasn't going to admit to him that she was free for the night, not even if he tied her up and tortured her. It would only complicate things.

Well, so much for willpower. All the man had to do was wrap his big, strong arms around her, flip the switch on his rugged male charm and let her think there was something personal about the steel rod that nudged her stomach. Lily's control gave a little whimper and then it melted like sealing wax.

When she closed her eyes, she could feel his breath on her cheek. The soft brush of his mustache, followed by the touch of his warm lips on her skin sent sensation arcing through her like a lightning bolt.

Though she was tempted, sorely tempted, to give in to what they both wanted, she had to remember that there were secrets she could never share with him. A truth that would make him despise her.

"This is a bad idea," she protested. "It would never work."

"I'm not asking for forever," he countered, "just a little piece of it. Don't expect me to keep ignoring the sparks we generate together— that we've always struck off each other. The difference is that now, we don't have to wait."

She swallowed a moan of disappointment. He couldn't know that leaving him had nearly broken her, or how close she was to falling for him all over again. If all he cared about was sampling what they had never shared with each other, what she wanted as much as he obviously did, why should she deny either of them at long last?

Without warning, he took her mouth in a hot, wet kiss that short-circuited her brain and left her clutching at his broad shoulders. Somewhere along the path of life, he'd certainly honed his skills in that department.

"But we—" she gasped when he broke the kiss, struggling to remember why she had decided this would be a bad idea.

"Haven't you been curious?" he demanded softly, cupping her breast through her blouse and flicking her nipple with his thumb so that she felt the rough caress right down to her core. "Don't you think I haven't wondered if I would have been enough…"

He broke off abruptly, but not before she felt a shudder go through him.

"Enough?" she echoed, but then she knew what he hadn't been willing to say—what he must believe of himself because of the way she had treated him.

That *he* hadn't been enough to keep her here.

She buried her face against his shoulder as regret burned through her like caustic acid. Why did life have to be so complex? He deserved more of an explanation than she'd given him; he deserved the truth that would free him forever. The truth that would turn the heat in his gaze to loathing.

If the right situation shoved itself in a man's face, those feelings wouldn't matter, she reminded herself. He could feel distaste on one level and still respond—still want—on another.

It wasn't fair or right to let him go on blaming himself. To think he'd failed in some way.

In order to get his attention, she captured his face between the palms of her hands. "I promise," she said earnestly, "it wasn't about you or anything you did. Please believe me."

His eyes narrowed and a muscle flexed in his cheek, but he didn't pull away.

"I wish I could say more," she continued carefully. "Please believe me when I tell you that I truly believed at the time that I had no other options. There was nothing that you—or anyone—could have done to change my mind." She tried to smile, but her lips trembled. "Don't blame yourself for failing me. I was the one who failed me."

He dropped his arms and turned away from her, one hand absently rubbing the back of his neck. She felt chilled all over, despite the warmth of the early evening air. In that moment she knew, without the slightest doubt, that anything she could do to rekindle his desire, short of telling him the truth, she would willingly do.

When he turned back around with a somber expression, she opened her arms. "I've made my decision," she said softly. "Now, what's yours?"

For an endless moment, he stared while she wished she could read his thoughts. When she was about to give up and lower her arms, he suddenly broke.

"Heaven help me, but I still can't resist you." He sounded almost angry as he swept her back into his arms. "Come to bed with me," he whispered against her lips.

Without giving her a chance to answer, he bent down and scooped her up. As he carried her through the house, nestled against his heart, she could feel it beating in tune with her own. Turning her head, she pressed her lips to the warm skin of his throat—and told herself that the next little while in his arms would be enough.

Chapter Nine

Convinced that Steve's intention was to satisfy a craving that began and ended with hormones, Lily expected to be tossed onto his king-size bed and to have her clothes stripped away like paint from a table—only faster. Instead, he stopped in the middle of the large room with its wall of windows framing the darkness. He held her effortlessly, as though she weighed no more than a feather pillow.

"On a clear morning, I like watching the sunrise," he said.

His voice rumbled against her ear, which was pressed against his chest. She thought he might ask her to stay, but he didn't. Too soon and way too dangerous for either of them.

"It must be a lovely view," she murmured.

His eyes crinkled at the outer corners when he smiled down at her. "Not half as pretty as what I'm looking at now."

He lowered his arm and let her slide down his body until her feet touched the floor. She had no choice but to put her arms around his neck to steady her shaky legs.

"You don't need to flatter me." She reached up to brush the hair back from his forehead. "I told you that I already made my decision." Over the years she had learned to deal with compliments about her appearance, but she'd figured out a long time ago that they usually came with strings. Something expected in exchange, but she didn't want to play that game with Steve.

He grabbed her hand, startling her. "You don't really know me anymore, so I won't take offense," he told her, "but you'll figure out in time that I don't care for lies, not even little white fibs, so I don't say what I don't mean." He lifted her hand and kissed the back of it. "Just accept the truth that you're still the most beautiful woman that I've ever seen."

She had no idea what to say in response to

his comment. It pained her to think she no longer knew him as she once had, better than anyone else. Then he turned her hand and pressed his open mouth to her palm. Words no longer seemed to matter as his tongue traced a path to the inside of her wrist. The fingers of her free hand tightened in the hair at his nape and she leaned into the hard length of his body. He lifted his head. The glow from the lamp turned the planes of his face to polished bronze and his blue eyes to softly glowing jewels.

"We've waited a long time for this," he said, voice rough. "I don't want to disappoint you."

Once again he stunned her by admitting something she hadn't expected. A wave of tenderness threatened to bring tears to her eyes. To stop them, she focused on the anticipation that had brought her to this point.

"There's no way you could do that," she replied, briefly touching her hand to his cheek. She had no idea how much of her current desire stemmed from the remembered frustration of resisting temptation when they were teens, nor did she care. She was finally here, about to make love with this sexy, attractive man who appealed to her on so many levels. "I worry, too," she added. "It's been a long time for me."

She hadn't meant to admit that last part,

even though it was true. Except for a couple of unsuccessful attempts at finding companionship and a few meaningless physical encounters, she had spent her time raising Jordan, attending school and managing Francis's accounts.

Steve tipped back her head and pressed an achingly gentle kiss to her mouth. Unless he ramped up the pace, she would end up begging him to take her.

In order to shift the mood and turn up the heat, she traced the shape of his lips with the tip of her tongue, then quickly retreated when he attempted to return the caress. He growled deep in his throat, then nibbled on her lips until she could no longer resist. When she yielded to him, he ravished her with a thoroughness that banished any thoughts about moving too slow. While she attempted to catch her breath, he shifted his attention to the sensitive skin of her throat. Deliberately, he brushed his knuckles over her swollen nipple before undoing the first button of her blouse.

She arched her back to grant him more access, which nestled her lower body intimately against him. He released her just long enough to yank his shirt over his head. She finished unbuttoning her blouse and let it drop to the floor. While he dealt with her bra, she explored his muscular chest with hands that trembled. He cupped her breasts, squeezing gently to send fresh pleasure surging through her. The feel of his work-roughened fingers made her bite her lip to muffle a moan of enjoyment.

"Did I hurt you?" he demanded.

She pressed her face against the hot skin of his shoulder. "Oh, no, no, no. Nothing has ever felt so good." She turned her head to caress his nipple with her tongue, pleased at his sharp intake of breath.

"I wanted to go slow," he said into her hair, "but my self-control has left the building."

"Then don't," she told him, breathing in the scent of his skin. "Don't hold back."

He caught her mouth in a searing kiss, and then she felt his fingers at the waistband of her jeans. He slid them and her panties over her hips as she fumbled with his belt. Obviously, he was much more experienced at undressing a member of the opposite sex, because she was buck naked before she had managed to unfasten his jeans.

"Here, let me." Brushing aside her suddenly inept fingers, he dealt with the rest of his clothes while her brain took a side trip to wonder if he would approve of her body. Then he straightened back up and her heart nearly stopped at the sight of him.

He was big and strong, more mesmerizing than a male centerfold. Unable to resist, she slid her hand down his flat stomach. Before she could reach her goal, he gripped her waist and tossed her lightly onto the mattress. She'd barely landed when he followed her down.

"Blame this on thirteen years of anticipation," he said as he slid his hand between her parted thighs. "And not one minute longer."

When his fingers touched her moist flesh, her body arched upward in welcome.

"Wait, just wait." He rolled away and she heard a drawer slide open, but a moment later he was back. As though a silent agreement had been reached, she parted her legs and he slid into her in one long stroke. The shock of invasion turned to an explosion of sensation as he held himself rigidly still, arms braced.

As natural as breathing, she wrapped herself around him and held on tight.

"Sweet, sweet Lily," he whispered, and then he began to move.

Everything about the two of them together was new to her, and yet familiar as he drove her up, up until she hovered, struggling to wait, desperate to soar. "Hurry," she gasped. "I can't, I can't—" And then she had no choice but to let go and fly. With his cheek against her hair, he joined her.

"Stay the night, what's left of it," he urged later, after they had made love a second time and she was nearly too limp to move.

"I'd better not," she murmured, worried about overstaying her welcome.

He nuzzled her ear. "I'll serve you a great breakfast."

She could feel his smile against her neck and she didn't figure he was referring to toast and coffee. All she wanted was to cuddle up to him and let herself go under, the idea so tempting that it scared her.

"I have to go." When she attempted to sit up, he hooked an arm around her waist and pulled her back against him.

"I won't let you," he whispered. "Not again."

Was there a message behind his words or were they merely just something to say? She had no idea, so she forced out a chuckle.

"I have duties and obligations," she said lightly. "Unfortunately, breakfast with you isn't one of them."

His arm fell away, leaving her chilled, and

he switched the lamp on low against the darkness. "I wish I could change your mind," he said, but he was already flipping back the covers.

As he swung his legs over the side of the bed, she wanted to say, *you could try.* Instead she sat up, sheet held modestly against her breasts. "I'm glad you understand." She hadn't done mornings like this in so long that she'd forgotten the protocol.

It was probably *leave quickly and don't make a fuss.*

Clearly at ease with his own nudity, Steve came around to her side of the bed and sat on the edge of the mattress. Leaning closer, he kissed her lightly while she wished she could read his thoughts. "Just because I understand doesn't mean that I like the idea," he said. "It's the middle of the night, so I'll follow you home."

Nothing could have touched her more deeply. "No, that's not necessary," she protested as he picked up the jeans he'd discarded earlier and slid them on. "I'll be fine."

When he turned away, she flipped aside the covers and grabbed her underwear. After scooting into them in record time, she picked up her blouse and shook it out.

Steve had already pulled on his shirt.

"Really, you don't have to follow me," she insisted as he fastened his belt.

His gaze was narrowed, his piercing expression giving her a glimpse of the side she hadn't seen before. No wonder he was able to boss around a crew of big, tough construction workers. "Not negotiable." He sounded like a drill sergeant. "Save your breath."

Her mouth dropped open.

"Bathroom's in there," he added with a jab of his thumb. "I'll meet you in the kitchen."

Trust him to turn a thoughtful gesture into an arrogant command, she fumed as she made use of the facilities and finger-combed her hair in the oval mirror above the etched glass sink. At least his abrupt attitude change had snapped her fuzzy brain back into reality mode.

When she left the bathroom, she hesitated in order to give herself a moment. For the first time, she really noticed the dimly lit bedroom. In addition to the wide bed that faced the wall of windows were a pair of nightstands and a tall dresser. All three were made of some dark wood that had been polished to gleam softly. She was no expert, but in the glow from the small lamp, the pieces looked handmade.

As she pulled on her jeans, she noticed that

except for the tangle of bedding that trailed onto the shag rug, the room was scrupulously neat. A single picture decorated one wall, a framed print of a cowboy standing in the snow. From one gloved hand dangled a leather harness. On the dresser beneath it was a bronze sculpture of a horse and rider.

Lily found one sandal, but the other eluded her. Finally she spotted it under the bed where she'd apparently kicked it.

"Looking for dust bunnies?" Steve drawled from the doorway when she was still on her hands and knees. "My service vacuumed last week."

She grabbed the sandal and scrambled to her feet. "And I can say firsthand that they're doing an excellent job," she replied as she slipped on the sandal without quite meeting his eyes. Odd that she'd been fine when he was nude, but now that he wore clothes, she felt self-conscious.

Wouldn't a shrink have fun with that?

"Still determined to leave?" he asked. "Or you could give me the fun of undressing you again. I always did enjoy unwrapping pretty packages."

His comment reminded her of the times they had exchanged little gifts for birthdays or other occasions. He'd never ripped off the paper as she had, preferring to lengthen the anticipation instead—and driving her crazy with waiting to see his delight.

"I think you've had enough fun for one night." She expected him to move out of the doorway so she could leave the room, but instead he stayed rooted there like a Douglas fir.

When she finally looked into his face, he was frowning. "Just for the record, this wasn't just a roll in the hay," he said, sounding annoyed. "Not to me."

She was dying to ask what he meant, but she didn't want to pressure him into coming up with some trite explanation that would only disappoint her. "Me, neither," she admitted when he still didn't move.

To her surprise, he cupped her chin in his fingers. "When will I see you again?"

Her nerve endings responded to his touch as though he had caressed her most intimate flesh. "At the office in a few hours." She tried to sound flippant, dismayed by the fresh wave of desire pouring through her, as hot as molten lava and stronger now that she knew how it felt to be possessed by him.

"Let me take you to dinner tomorrow night," he said with a smile. "There's a great restaurant in Sequim that I think you'll like."

Again he'd managed to surprise her, but she had to refuse. "Have you forgotten that I have a son?" If Jordan was going to be a problem, she wanted to know now.

She expected Steve to suggest that she hire a sitter, but instead his grin widened. "I know he likes pizza, so let's all go to Bella's."

"You can't come back to my house and wait around for him to fall asleep afterward," she warned him. "I can't do that."

Steve looked shocked. "Give me a little credit. I'll bet I can control my base nature for one evening."

She flushed, thoroughly embarrassed by her own presumptions. "I didn't mean, uh—" she stumbled, face burning.

With a chuckle, he reached for her. "Relax, honey," he said into her hair after he'd wrapped his arms around her. "If it was up to me, we wouldn't leave this room for a month, maybe longer. That doesn't mean I don't realize you have obligations." He slid his hand underneath her hair to lightly grip the back of her neck. "It's cool with me, okay? We'll play it by ear."

"Thank you," she mumbled into his chest.

"Meanwhile, how does pizza sound?" he persisted.

* * *

"You're a good sport," Lily told Steve as they sat across the table from each other at Bella's the next evening. "You didn't sign on for feeding *two* growing boys." Cory's mother had called to ask if Lily would mind taking him for the evening. Steve had refused her attempt to cancel dinner with him.

He shrugged, but his mustache failed to hide his grin. "It's hard to be Mr. Romance when you've got chaperones. Maybe that's not entirely a bad thing," he added enigmatically.

Wishing he had time to elaborate, Lily watched the boys weave a path through the other tables on their way back from the restroom. At least Cory seemed like a good kid and she liked his parents.

"Isn't the food here yet?" Jordan exclaimed, dropping back into his chair dramatically. "I'm starving."

"Me, too," Cory chimed. "Hey, did you hear that Ryan got a webcam for his computer? That's so cool. I'm going to ask my dad for one."

Jordan looked at Lily. "Could I—"

"Nope," she replied before he'd finished.

"How do you even know what I'm going to

ask?" he demanded, slumping as though he'd been shot. "You always say no."

"There are people on the Web that I don't want to see you," Lily replied.

"Not everyone out there is a friend," Steve added.

As she gave him a grateful glance, Bella herself brought over a huge tray with their pizzas. She was followed by her pretty, dark-haired granddaughter, who carried their drinks. Lily had to stifle a smile when she saw the way both boys eyed Gina while pretending to look the other way. Steve winked at Lily, indicating that he, too, had noticed.

"How nice to see you all again," Bella boomed out in her loud, cheerful voice as she set down the tray and unloaded it. She clapped a reddened hand on Steve's shoulder. "Just like a family, eh?"

Lily considered sliding down in her chair until she was hidden by the red-checkered tablecloth. "Bella, you still serve the best pizza in town," she said, desperate to distract the older woman. "Gina, are you looking forward to your senior year?"

Twin dimples flashed when the young girl smiled. "I made the cheer squad."

"Congratulations," Lily told her. "You'll have a lot of fun."

"Fun!" Bella echoed scornfully, rolling her eyes. "School is for learning, for education, not *fun*." She managed to make the word sound like a social disease.

"Cheerleading is great exercise," Steve said, surprising Lily. "A healthy body is as important as a healthy mind."

Jordan managed to turn a snort of laughter into a cough. Lily gave him a quelling glance, vowing to have a little discussion with him later about girls and respect. It was times like this that she wished there was someone to share the task of raising a boy on the verge of adolescence. Wade was great for taking an interest, but having certain kinds of talks with her son certainly wasn't his responsibility.

Bella tipped her head to the side, considering Steve's comment. "Maybe you're right," she said, hand pressed to her ample bosom. "I hadn't thought of that. Come, Gina," she beckoned. "Let's allow these nice folks to eat before their pies get cold."

Behind her grandmother's back, Gina mouthed a silent *thank you* to Steve. "I'll check back on you later," she added aloud.

"I think you've made a new fan," Lily told him.

"That makes two this week," he drawled with a knowing grin.

"You wish," she muttered, conscious of her son sitting beside her as they all helped themselves to the pizza.

"Mom, do Cory and I look like brothers?" he asked between bites.

Lily glanced at the two boys, one fair and the other with brown hair and freckles. "You could be twins. Why do you ask?"

"Just wondering," he replied with a shrug.

For the next few moments, the table was relatively silent as they ate. While Lily sipped her diet cola, she tried to analyze his question.

Did he miss having siblings? A stepfather? Was she being unfair? But what choice did she have? There wasn't a superstore where one could shop for that kind of thing.

"I hope it's not my taxes that are putting those creases in your forehead," Steve said quietly, watching her with a concerned expression.

His comment made her realize that she'd been staring at her plate without seeing it. She glanced at the boys, but they were deep into a discussion of the latest Harry Potter movie.

"I was just thinking about the future," she told Steve.

His brows rose upward. "That's a heavy subject, as well as a broad one. Care to be more specific?"

"Maybe later." Unless he'd had enough and planned to shove them out of his car, a late-model sedan she hadn't even realized he possessed, she should probably invite him in for coffee when he took them back to her house. "Did the sale on your house go through?" she asked curiously. Surely taking time to help her and Wade must detract from his own business.

Steve helped himself to another slice. "It's supposed to close next week, and so far it looks like a go."

When Steve trailed after her and the boys into her house a little while later, he was resigned to the fact that there would be no opportunity for a repeat of the night before. He would just have to settle for a good-night kiss after the boys were settled.

"Thanks for the pizza, Steve," Jordan said.

"Yeah, thanks a lot," echoed his friend, Cory.

"You're both welcome," Steve replied, impressed with their manners.

Lily hadn't mentioned that Cory would be spending the night until Steve arrived earlier to pick them up. Apologetically, she had tried to slip him some money toward the pizza, but he'd refused.

"We're going to play in my room," Jordan told Lily.

"Just don't make a lot of noise," she told the boys as they disappeared down the hallway.

"Have a seat," she told Steve. "I'll be right back."

He sat on the floral-printed couch that he'd first seen when he helped move her into this house. The room looked different, more homey, but he wasn't sure what she'd done to change it.

All the way into town this morning to begin tearing out the bathroom at the office redo, he had looked forward to seeing her. Video images of hot sex on the kitchen counter and the bedroom floor streamed through his head—until he'd pulled into the driveway and Jordan shot out the front door to greet him.

"I thought you'd never get here!" he exclaimed, replacing sexual fantasy with the complexities of real life.

Jordan was a good kid, though, curious and smart. He did everything Steve asked without complaint, whether it was running out to the truck for some tool or sweeping up shavings from the floor. Steve figured that hanging with him had something to do with being raised without a father. Some schmuck was missing out on a great kid.

"You want some coffee?" Lily asked when she reappeared. "It will only take a minute to make."

"That'd be my second choice," he drawled, just to see her reaction.

"Coffee's the only thing on tonight's menu," she retorted, heading for the kitchen.

Jordan had closed the door to his bedroom and Steve hadn't heard it reopen. When he caught up with Lily, he couldn't resist crowding her into the corner so he could drop a quick kiss onto her soft lips. She looked suitably flustered when he released her, but he didn't escape unscathed as every cell in his being clamored for more.

"Behave yourself!" she hissed.

He shoved his hands into his pockets and retreated. "Yes, ma'am."

While she made the coffee, he finally realized that even though the owner's furniture was still in place, a lot of the accessories that added to the cluttered appearance of the open rooms had been removed.

When he walked back into the kitchen, she grabbed a wooden spoon from a pot full of utensils on the counter.

"Be careful, I'm armed," she warned as she brandished it. "There are two impressionable boys just down the hall."

"Is that spoon loaded?" he asked, maintaining a safe distance.

Lily started to laugh. "I have no idea." She was still chuckling when she got mugs from the cupboard.

"Black, right?"

"Sounds good." He tried not to read any significance into the fact that she must have noticed and remembered. "I miss the artificial plants and the dried flowers."

She spun around, but when she saw his grin, she relaxed. "Isn't it enough that I have to live with ruffles and prints on every available surface?" she demanded with a sweeping gesture. "Jordan's a good kid, but he's still a kid and all those knickknacks made me nervous, so I packed a lot of them up. They're in the garage."

He leaned his shoulder against the door frame and watched while she arranged some chocolate chip cookies on two plates and then handed one to him with some napkins.

"Would you take these to the boys and tell them not to make a mess."

Steve sniffed appreciatively. "Homemade?" he guessed hopefully.

"You betcha. Baking relaxes me," she replied.

He could remember her cutting Home Ec back in school, so he was pleasantly surprised. When he returned, conveying the boys' appreciation, she poured coffee into two mugs and set them on the small table with the other plate. After he held out her chair, he seated himself.

"To second choices," he said, hoisting his mug.

Her smile seemed to grow wider. "And the men we bake for," she replied.

A feeling of contentment stole over him, so different from being alone at his house. How long had it been since he had last felt this relaxed, or had he ever?

"Tell me about your wife," she suggested as he took a big bite out of his cookie. "I don't think I knew her."

He shook his head as he chewed, debating just how much to say. "Christie worked at the lumberyard in Kingston, but she was from Tacoma." He didn't often think about that part of his life. No one liked dwelling on their failures.

Lily didn't comment as she sipped her coffee. Before he quite realized what was happening, he started talking.

"She was a sweet, decent woman who wanted nothing more out of life than a home and a family," he said. "Last I heard, she's got that now." He remembered his jumble of feelings when he'd run into her with a child in tow, another in her belly and her husband's hand in hers.

"I'm sorry that it didn't work out," Lily said softly.

He tried not to think about the reasons it hadn't. Before he could come up with a neutral comment, a door opened and footsteps came thudding toward the kitchen.

"Mom, can we have some more cookies?"

For a long time after Steve had left and the boys were finally asleep, Lily sat on the living-room couch in the dark. She had searched his face for some sign of frustrated desire when he left, but he seemed satisfied with the two cookies he'd taken for the road.

"I've got meetings all day tomorrow, but I'll

try to stop by," he told her after another quick kiss at the door. "Be sure to lock up after me." A moment later, she heard him drive away.

When her cell phone rang, her first thought as she shot off the couch was for Jordan before she realized he was safe in his room. She dug her cell phone from her purse and glanced at the screen.

"Forget something?" she asked.

"Can you get a sitter tomorrow night?" Steve demanded.

"I can try." A surge of happiness caught her off guard. "What did you have in mind?"

"Come to my house and we'll figure it out."

For a moment she was silent as she savored the dark, smoky tone of his voice.

"Lily?" he asked. "Are you there?"

"I'm here," she said softly, fingers tightening on her phone.

"Just so you know, I really, really want to come back right now. I won't do it, but I want to."

Longing hummed through her. "I'll get a sitter," she whispered.

Without another word, he clicked off. What else was there to say? His meaning was crystal clear.

Chapter Ten

As Lily drove out to Steve's house the next evening after taking Jordan to the Burger Shack for supper, she tried not to think about the reason for her visit. If she had a working brain, she would turn the car around and go back home.

She told herself that it would be too awkward to explain to both Jordan and his sitter, Bertie Hemplemann, why she was back so soon. Bertie was an older woman who worked part-time in Pauline's cross-stitch shop. Lily had met Bertie on several occasions. Jordan liked her and she always offered to stay with him whenever Lily might need someone. Tonight, Bertie had arrived with an armload of board games.

Jordan's enthusiasm helped to ease the guilt Lily felt for the stumbling excuse she'd made for not taking him with her tonight so he could see the dogs again. She'd told him that she and Steve needed to go over his taxes. Technically, it wasn't a lie, but she had already finished his return.

As Lily drove past a double-wide mobile home next to a cow pasture, she decided to buy Jordan the video game he wanted to make up for not taking him tonight.

Despite the nagging of her conscience, she felt a shiver of anticipation when she rounded a bend in the two-lane road and saw Steve's house. In moments, she would be alone with him.

She had missed him today. Working at the office wasn't the same without him, but twice he had taken the time between meetings with subcontractors and a county inspector to make sure she was still coming. Although he'd been all business on the phone, he sounded relieved to hear that she hadn't changed her mind.

As she pulled into the circular driveway and parked behind his truck, she finally allowed the thought to form in her head. She was going to sleep with him again.

Never before in her life had she experienced such an intense feeling of expectation. A physical response already sizzled inside her and she could hardly wait to see him.

When she got out of her car and saw him standing on the porch with his arms folded across his broad chest and his jeans molded to his long muscular legs, she thought she might collapse right there in front of him. A sudden attack of nerves made her want to bolt and yet she was helpless to resist the pull of attraction.

Wordlessly, he came down the steps, wearing such an intense expression on his face that she thought something must be wrong. Perhaps Bertie had called. Lily had left her the number, as well as her own cell phone's, but the signals were notoriously unreliable around here.

Calm down, she ordered herself silently. If there was anything wrong, he would tell her. She opened her mouth, but no sound came out as she stared up at him with helpless fascination.

"Lily," he breathed as he took her in his arms and kissed her with the same intensity she felt toward him. The cheerful honk of a passing car barely penetrated the red mist swirling in her head as she clung to him. By the time he let her go, she was trembling all over.

His face was flushed, his gaze predatory. "This has been the longest day of my life," he said hoarsely, curving his arm around her shoulders as he led her inside.

"Me, too," Lily admitted, handing him the tax return.

"Thanks."

He kicked the front door shut behind them and she dropped her bag to the floor. Tossing the papers onto a table, he backed her against the wall, hands braced on either side of her.

"Do you want a glass of wine?" he asked.

When she shook her head slowly with her gaze locked on his, he leaned down and kissed her again. She moaned against his open mouth, afraid she would go up in flames. She couldn't get close enough as she buried one hand in his hair and wrapped the other around his waist. She arched up so her breasts were flattened against his chest and her hips nudged his arousal.

"You're hot enough to melt glass," he groaned as he lifted her into his arms. Quickly he walked down the hallway.

"I hope we don't burn down the house," she murmured distractedly against the hot skin of his throat. She inhaled the pleasant scents of soap and cologne, pleased that he had show-ered and shaved for her.

"If we burn it down, I'll build another one." When he got to his bedroom, he set her onto her feet and peeled his shirt over his head. Distracted by the sight of his bare chest, Lily unbuttoned her blouse. As soon as they had finished undressing, he yanked the covers off the bed and tumbled her onto the wide expanse.

He lay on his back and she took advantage, straddling his hard thighs so she could run her hands over the firm planes of his chest. While she sifted her fingers through the patch of gold hair between his flat nipples, teasing him, he cupped her breasts and did some tor-menting of his own.

He skated his fingers down her stomach and she rocked forward against his hand as the need throbbed through her.

"Sweet, sweet Lily," he murmured. Nudg-ing her over, he lifted up and turned away for a moment. When he rose over her, bracing his weight on his elbow, she welcomed him with a thankful sigh and gave herself up to him. Like a chain reaction, her surrender sparked his. Clinging together, they took the last long step off the cliff and plunged.

Moments later, she lay cuddled against him

as her heartbeat slowly returned to normal—
as normal as it got when she was around him.

"Good thing I had time to do a little shopping," he murmured, stroking her hair. "Do
you remember Mr. Roderick? He's working
at the drugstore now."

"You bought condoms from our high-school
math teacher?" she exclaimed on a gurgle of
laughter. "Did he remember you?"

"Oh, yeah," Steve drawled. "He said to tell
you hi."

Lily jerked her head around so she could
see his face. "You've got to be kidding!" she
cried. "I'll never be able to shop there again."

"Had you going for a minute, huh?" His
eyes were full of unrepentant laughter. "How
long can you stay with me?"

She glanced at the clock radio on his night-
stand, tempted to tell him they were supposed
to be going over his taxes. Then she remembered how he felt about lying, even little white
fibs. "The sitter told me not to hurry home."

His mouth curved into a sexy smile. "This
time we'll take it real, real slow."

By the time his powerful body trembled
with his release, he had wrung every last bit
of passion from her that she possessed. As he

collapsed beside her, she lay with her arms flung outward, as limp as a rag doll.

"I'll be lucky if I can move before morning," she grumbled, surrounded by lengthening shadows.

He kissed her cheek gently. "Honey, you can stay as long as you want. Judy will just have to dust around us."

"Judy?" she echoed suspiciously.

"Relax. She's my cleaning lady, comes in once a week to shovel out the place while I'm at work." He flopped over onto his back. "She's a blessing."

Lily managed to prop herself up on one elbow. "I'm feeling a little stronger now," she whispered, planting a kiss on his chest.

He tucked a strand of her hair behind her ear. "Ready for a glass of that wine?"

She could have studied his ruggedly handsome face for an hour. Instead she sneaked another glance at the clock, amazed at how quickly the time flew by when she was with him. "I'd better stick to coffee, if it's not too much trouble."

He sat up and swung his legs over the side of the bed. "How about a shower first? I'll let you wash my back."

The embers of desire she thought were

thoroughly banked suddenly burst into life. She had never been especially passionate, but now she couldn't seem to get enough.

"Only if you wash mine," she retorted. Leaning back on her elbows, she watched him walk buck naked toward the master bath. He must have realized that she hadn't stirred, because he looked over his shoulder.

"What?" he asked.

"Just enjoying the eye candy," she said with a teasing grin.

"Oh, yeah?" Face reddening, he leaned one broad shoulder against the door frame and beckoned to her. "My turn. Come and join me, little lady."

Feeling surprisingly self-conscious considering how thoroughly they had explored each other's bodies, she met his challenging grin with what she hoped was a smoldering glance of her own as she peeled back the sheet and got to her feet. Arms at her sides, she crossed the room, which suddenly seemed to have grown to the length of a football field.

He watched her intently, unable to hide his swift reaction. His hands were gratifyingly unsteady when she reached him and he cupped her jaw. Thumbs urging her lips apart, he kissed her deeply. Then he captured her hand in his and led her into the spacious shower. It wasn't until he was seated beneath the spray with her straddling him, straining to get even closer, that she recalled what they'd forgotten.

"We didn't—" she gasped as his hands clamped on her thighs. She waved her arm in the direction of the bedroom as sensation rippled through her. "You should probably stop and—" A fresh wave of passion stole her breath and her ability to speak.

"I'm clean," he said against her breath. "You?"

She nodded, struggling to think. "Pregnancy," she managed to whisper.

"You're safe with me." His hands tightened and his shoulders went rigid.

Unable to think, she lost her grip on reality as he thrust back his head, jaw clenched, and they soared.

After they dried each other off with big fluffy towels, Lily finished dressing while Steve slipped on a pair of sweatpants that rode dangerously low on his hips.

"I'll go make the coffee," he said with a lingering glance.

When she joined him in the kitchen, he

held up two tickets. Behind him on the counter, the coffee made brewing noises.

"What're those?" she asked curiously.

"Mariners baseball," he said with a grin. "Day after tomorrow. Want to come?"

It sounded like fun, but she already had plans. "I can't. I'm attending a bridal shower for Pauline."

His smile faded, but then he snapped his fingers. "I'll bet I know a kid who'd like to go with me. What do you think? Ferry ride, hot dogs, great seats? Sound good?"

Gratitude flooded through her. "Sounds terrific," she agreed.

"I'll check the ferry schedule and let you know," he said as he poured the coffee.

"What did you mean back there?" Lily asked after they'd sat at the table. "You said I was safe." He couldn't possibly have had a vasectomy, not at his age.

His jaw tightened and he flushed, but he didn't reply until after he'd taken a drink from his oversized mug with Brown's Plumbing printed on the side. When he looked at her, resignation had replaced his appearance of lazy satisfaction.

"I seriously doubt I could get you pregnant," he said bluntly. "I was married for three years and we never used anything, but now she's popping out kids like gum balls. It's not hard to do the math."

"Have you talked to anyone?" Lily asked, reaching across the table to link her fingers with his.

He scrubbed his free hand over his face. "Naw. Since we separated, there's been no real reason."

She figured the truth he wasn't saying was that he didn't want to know for sure. Even the possibility had to be devastating for such a virile man as Steve. For any man.

"We should use something until I get back on the pill," she said, partly as a test to see what he would say. Did he figure they would keep sleeping together until one of them got bored, or was he beginning to care for her again?

He shrugged. "I don't want you to worry. Look, if I'm wrong and there should be any… consequences, we'll face them together. You have to promise that you'll tell me, though. No running away."

Moved by everything he had told her, she could only nod in agreement before taking a gulp of her coffee. Lucky for her, it had cooled or she would have scalded her tongue without even noticing. She wanted to tell him that his suspicions didn't matter, not to her, but he would probably misinterpret her meaning. Besides, it wasn't her place to comment. Not yet, and maybe not ever.

Steve spent most of the next day catching up on his own work. While he waited for the truck to deliver his plumbing fixtures, he sat at a card table in the three-car garage and tinkered with a set of building specs on his laptop.

Wade had his doctor's go-ahead to use his wrist "in moderation" and he was more than capable of supervising the crew refinishing the hardwood floors. The asphalt guys were also coming to pave an area on the side of the building to avoid street parking as much as possible.

Lily was in charge of landscaping the front yard while the house was full of dust and fumes. She'd mentioned going to the nursery this morning with Pauline.

Perhaps Steve would drive by later to see how things were going. Until he received the delayed permit, he couldn't begin the next project, so he'd given his crew the week off. He'd been promised the permit next week for sure and he was eager to get started. Meanwhile, unable to concentrate, he shut down the laptop and got to his feet.

Images of Lily and the way they'd spent a good chunk of last night stirred an instant reaction that altered the fit of his jeans. She was every man's erotic fantasy: gorgeous, sexy and hot enough to set his hair on fire. When he wasn't reliving their last encounter, he was plotting the next.

She had insisted on staying home tonight in order to spend some time with her son. Tomorrow, she was going to a wedding shower that one of Pauline's customers was throwing.

One of Steve's suppliers had given him the pair of tickets to the Mariners game over at Safeco Field. Free caps would be given to kids twelve and under, so Steve was taking Jordan to see the game. Picking him up would give Steve an excuse to see Lily, if only briefly.

How pathetic was that? he asked himself as the truck with the plumbing fixtures rumbled down the long driveway. He was acting like a man going down for the count.

Shaking off the notion, he tripped over a can of paint sitting in the middle of the garage floor. Cursing loudly, he went sprawling onto the concrete.

* * *

"You've been rather quiet today," Pauline told Lily as the two of them left the bridal shower. "Don't tell me you're not into playing silly games, eating cake and watching someone else open a stack of presents."

Lily rubbed her temple, where a headache was beginning to throb. "Mavis did a nice job with the decorations and everything," she said diplomatically as they got into Pauline's car and she unpinned her corsage made from the package bows. "The Hawaiian wedding theme was cute, even if she did have to play that song over and over."

"I kept waiting for an Elvis impersonator to jump out at any moment," Pauline agreed, "but everyone seemed to have a good time." She glanced at Lily as she drove down the street. "Everyone except you," she amended. "What gives?"

Lily debated how much to say, but Pauline was her sister and the need to confide in someone was practically overwhelming. "I'm sleeping with Steve," she blurted.

Pauline hit the brakes a little too hard when she stopped for a red light. "Are you trying to get us killed?" she demanded. "Telling me something like that without warning! How long has this been going on?"

Lily bristled. "I'm not asking for your blessing!"

Pauline immediately reached over and patted Lily's hand, which was balled into a fist in her lap. "I'm sorry," she said gently. "You just caught me by surprise, that's all, but I didn't mean to give the impression that I'm not happy about it."

She glanced again at Lily, who was beginning to wish she'd kept her big mouth shut. "*You*, on the other hand, don't look exactly blissful, if I may say so," Pauline said quietly.

Lily slunk down in the passenger seat. "It's complicated," she muttered. "I don't know how I feel."

An irritating smile crossed Pauline's face as she looked straight ahead. "Well, I assume that you must like him a little bit or you wouldn't be boinking him, right?"

Lily's mouth fell open at her conservative sister's comment. *"Boinking?"* she echoed with a gurgle of reluctant laughter. "Is that what you and your fiancé have been doing, boinking?"

"We're not talking about me right now," Pauline replied, cheeks slightly pink. "I want to know all the details, sister dear. When did you get back together? Are you serious about him?"

Lily rolled her eyes. Leave it to Pauline to attempt to analyze everything.

"That sly dog," Pauline mused as she drove along the top of the bluff through one of the older sections of town. The street was lined with gorgeous old mansions built by the local lumber barons of the 1890s. "He never let on."

"Let's pick up your invitations," Lily suggested, eager to change the subject. "We've got to go right past the supplier." Pauline had ordered matching cards and envelopes of marbled paper.

"Good idea," Pauline replied. "After I print off the script on the computer, you can help me with the inserts I stitched. Even though everyone pretty much knows about it already, I want to get them in the mail." She shook her head, expression soft with wonder. "It's hard to believe that we're getting married in a little over a month. I don't know how people survive planning big weddings."

"How many people are you inviting?" Lily asked as they parked on the street.

"No more than will fit in the parlor if it rains," Pauline replied, rolling her eyes.

While she went to pick up her order, Lily waited in the SUV. The last thing she wanted was to be jealous of her own sister, but sometimes she caught herself wondering whether she and Steve would have gotten married if she hadn't succumbed to Carter's smarmy charms.

Shock rippled through her when she realized that without him there would be no Jordan. She couldn't imagine life without her son, but she'd never thought much about having more children.

Since her conversation with Steve, she'd come to realize that she liked being able to focus on one child. Having another, especially a little girl, would be nice, but it wasn't a dealbreaker. Not if it came to a choice between that and a man she loved.

The driver's door opened, startling Lily from her thoughts.

"You look as though you're trying to solve the world's problems," Pauline exclaimed when she slid behind the wheel. "What are you thinking about with such concentration?"

Lily wouldn't feel right in sharing Steve's confidence. "Nothing much," she replied. "Let's see the cards."

Carefully Pauline lifted the cover from the

box. Inside was the thick handmade paper she had special-ordered, creamy white with a faint marble pattern.

"That's really pretty." Lily took a closer look. "With all our modern technology, people are still making paper by hand."

As Pauline replaced the lid, Lily's cell phone rang from inside her purse.

"It's Steve," she said after checking the display. "I hope everything's okay."

There was a lot that Steve would have liked to tell Lily, but he couldn't say much with her son sitting across from him on the ferry back from Seattle. Instead, he handed the ringing phone to Jordan.

"Tell your mom hi for me." While Steve tested his resistance, he stared out the big side window of the ferry at the choppy blue water and the seagulls circling above it. Every few moments, one of them would dive-bomb into the water after a fish. He knew from previous experience that they could also pick popcorn from the air when it was tossed from the outside deck.

With one ear he listened to Jordan's enthusiastic rendition of their day while the other part of him wondered how Lily felt about what he'd told her. Other than reducing any worries she might have had about an unplanned pregnancy, she probably didn't care one way or the other about his possible sterility.

His mind shied away from the word and he focused on Jordan's end of the phone conversation.

"The Safe—that's what they call Safeco Field—is awesome," he said. "We had seats right behind right field and Steve bought hot dogs. I had two and they were better than anything I've ever tasted. Oh, and I got a cool cap. It's got a team logo, a trident, on the front, and they gave one to every kid who came through the gates."

Steve smothered a grin as Jordan rambled on. He was a good kid and a surprisingly entertaining companion. If the locals insisted on crediting Steve with fathering a child, he could have done a lot worse.

He refused to speculate on the identity of the boy's biological father, preferring to wait for Lily to volunteer the information. He wondered, though, why any man would prefer not to be involved in his son's life. If Jordan really had been Steve's, he would have insisted on it.

"I don't know," Jordan said, glancing up

at him. "I'll ask." He covered the phone with his hand. "Mom wants to know when we'll be back. She and Aunt Pauline are going out for dinner."

Steve glanced at his watch and did some quick calculations. "Probably another hour and a half. Tell her we'll call again when we go through Kingston."

Jordan relayed the message. "She wants to talk to you."

At least she hadn't abandoned him entirely, he thought with a touch of black humor as he took back his phone.

"Hiya," he drawled, conscious of Jordan watching him like a hawk. "How was the shower?" He twirled his finger in a "big deal" gesture and Jordan giggled. A shared joke between guys about stupid girlie stuff.

"Pauline got some nice things," Lily replied. "I'm sure that Wade will appreciate the lingerie."

"Don't tell him that!"

Steve recognized her sister's voice. Obviously, Lily couldn't speak freely, either.

"We played games and there was even a miniature wedding cake with three tiers," Lily cooed as Pauline laughed.

"You'll have to tell me more about the

games," Steve murmured as Jordan gave him a questioning glance. "They might be fun."

"Are they board games like Bertie brought over?" Jordan asked.

"I'm going to hang up now," Lily threatened. "Paulie picked up the paper for the invitations and we're taking Chinese food back to her house so we can put them together."

"Wow, more fun," Steve exclaimed. "Is Wade going to help with those?" He heard her repeat his question to Pauline.

"Surprisingly, he's not." Lily infused her voice with disbelief. "Apparently, he's going to be hanging out at an establishment called the Crab Roast? Crab Post? Oh, the Crab *Pot*. Do you know it?" she teased. "It's rumored to be a dive down on the waterfront."

"I seem to have heard something about it," Steve replied with a chuckle. "Some interesting women have been known to show up there, so maybe I'll drop the kid here off at Video World and join him."

Jordan sat up straighter. "Video World? Where's that?" he demanded.

Steve shook his head. "I made it up," he said out of the side of his mouth.

The kid slumped back onto his seat, clearly disappointed.

"Ask him if he wants to spend the night at Cory's," Lily suggested. "If he does, you can drop him off at Pauline's and I'll run him home first."

Steve's spirits rose like a hot-air balloon. "I can take him, if you want."

"Take me where?" Jordan was obviously still annoyed by Steve's "Video World" comment.

"If he wants to go and you don't mind, he needs to stop by our house first. There's a spare key under the flower-pot on the front porch," Lily said. "Make sure he packs a change of underwear and his toothbrush."

"No problem." A suggestion rocketed through Steve's brain. Conscious of his audience, as well as hers, he merely asked her to hold on while he confirmed the plans with Jordan.

"I could understand if you're too tired after being gone all day," Steve told him.

"Heck, no." Obviously the boy's good mood had been restored. "I can show Cory my new cap."

"It's a go," Steve confirmed to Lily. "I'll call you after I've delivered him." He hoped her thoughts were heading in the same direction as his own.

Chapter Eleven

After Steve dropped Jordan off at his friend's house, he drove down the hill to the Crab Pot. Wade's truck was parked out front, so Steve pulled into an empty slot next to it. He walked through the door, nodded to Riley, the bouncer who guarded the entry with a perpetual expression of deep suspicion, and spotted Wade seated at the bar nursing a beer. Overhead, the television displayed a women's track tournament.

"Thought you'd be helping the girls make wedding invitations," Steve said as he sat down next to his friend.

"I flunked cut-and-paste in preschool,"

Wade replied with a chuckle. He reached for some pretzels from a nearby basket. "How was the game?"

"Schooner?" the bartender asked.

Steve nodded in reply. "The Mariners won three-two in the bottom of the ninth," he told Wade, pulling out some bills. "I think Jordan had a good time and he's crazy about his free cap."

The bartender set down his beer and pointed at Wade's half-empty glass.

"Hell, why not?" Wade said. "Thanks, Mike."

Steve took a long, satisfying drink. "Kid-sitting is thirsty work," he commented.

"So what do you think of him?" Wade asked curiously after Mike replaced his empty glass. "Half the town still thinks he's yours."

"He's a good kid." Steve took another long pull from his schooner. "Lily's done an amazing job with him." He eyed Wade curiously. "You got any theories?"

Wade sipped his beer with a thoughtful expression. "About his father?" he hedged.

He knew something; Steve was sure of it. If Lily had confided in Pauline, she might have told him.

"No, about the price of pickles," Steve snapped. "What do you think I'm talking about?" He didn't realize that his voice had risen until Riley stood up and gave him the fish eye.

"Problem, guys?" His voice sounded as though it came up from the bottom of an empty barrel.

Steve grinned and Wade held up his hands. "No problem," they said in unison. No one wanted to piss off the bouncer. There were stories about what Riley had done when he lost his temper. They might not have been true, but none of the patrons of the Crab Pot were stupid enough to test him.

"Good." Riley smiled back at them, revealing a missing tooth that local legend said he'd lost in a fight with a grizzly. It didn't matter that grizzlies weren't native to the Olympic Peninsula; what mattered was that Riley had obviously won, since he was still here.

"If you and Lily are getting serious, maybe you need to talk to her about Jordan," Wade suggested, lowering his voice.

"We're just having a little fun, that's all." Steve winced at the defensiveness in his tone. Hell, was it obvious that he couldn't leave her alone? He must look like a real chump after the way she'd treated him. "Can't a guy even look at a woman without everyone trying to put a tux on him?"

"Ah," Wade said, "so that's what they call it now, looking." Lightly he punched Steve's shoulder. "If you hurry up and pop the question, we could have a double wedding."

His taunting tone hit Steve all wrong as he downed the rest of his beer.

Wade looked startled as he slid off his stool. "Where are you going?" he demanded.

Steve didn't bother to reply as he stalked toward the door, feeling as though he wore a sign on his back that said *Jerk*.

"Hey!" Wade hollered after him as Riley held open the door.

"Don't even say it," Steve snarled as he passed the human hulk. He had to be out of his mind to challenge Riley, who could probably break him in half, but suddenly picking a fight seemed like a great idea. Even the probability of getting pounded into pulp didn't faze him and he was disappointed when the bouncer just laughed.

"Take it easy driving home."

Before Steve got to his truck, Wade hurried up behind him. "What's going on with you? You know damn well I was just ribbing you."

He made the mistake of grabbing Steve's arm, lighting the fuse to his anger.

Without conscious thought, he shot out his fist, barely missing Wade's jaw as he dodged the blow. "Are you nuts?" he exclaimed, blocking another jab with his arm. "What the hell is your problem?"

"Come on, man. Take a shot," Steve coaxed, dancing around him, feeling as though he'd explode with frustration as he beckoned Wade closer.

Instead of complying, Wade managed to grab Steve's forearm when he swung again, pinning it behind him. Briefly they struggled. Steve's fury drained away as quickly as it had risen, leaving him feeling even more like an idiot than before.

Wade must have felt the tension go out of him, because he slowly eased his grip. "You okay now?" he asked warily. "I don't need any chipped teeth in my wedding photos."

Steve hung his head, plowing his free hand through his hair. "Hell, I don't know what got into me." Embarrassed, he held out his hand. "Sorry."

Wade grasped it firmly. "No problem. Come on, let's take a walk."

Neither of them spoke as they rounded the

long, low building that housed the Crab Pot. Steve remembered the day he had been here with Lily. Now the sun had already disappeared behind the Olympic Mountains to the west and a light breeze blew in from the water, rippling its surface.

A boardwalk connected several docks that stuck out like bony fingers. Except for a couple of guys hosing off the deck of a fishing boat, the area was deserted.

Wade wandered out to a wood bench sitting near the end of a pier and Steve followed. The fresh air was clearing his brain of beer fumes, making him wonder why Wade's kidding had fired him up so much. Maybe it was because of his suspicion that Wade knew more about Lily than he let on.

Wade sat down on one end of the bench, legs stuck out in front of him. A gull cried in apparent annoyance, sounding like a whiny child as it flapped its wings and flew away from a nearby railing. The salt air mingled with the smells of deep-fried food from the tavern and diesel fumes from the nearby boat. Water lapped rhythmically against the pilings, covered with barnacles below the high-water line, and the *put-put* of an outboard motor drifted across the water.

"It's peaceful here," Wade said as he watched the fishermen.

"You miss San Francisco much?" Steve asked. Wade had only been in Crescent Cove for a few months.

"Maybe the city and my condo," he replied, "but I don't think about it much at all. Getting married and opening the office are what's important to me now." Idly, he picked at a splinter in the weathered wood of the bench. "A good woman, family, work you love, that's what matters, right?"

In the distance Steve could see a freighter heading up the Strait, probably from Seattle's deep-water port. It was probably going to somewhere in Asia or maybe up to Vancouver.

He knew that Wade was waiting for some kind of comment, but he had no idea where to begin. He'd had good women, Lily, Christie, but he'd lost them both and he wasn't sure why.

"Does it bug you that she already has a kid?" Wade asked.

"Hell, no," Steve replied without thinking. "I like Jordan. The whole raising-another-man's-child issue just wouldn't be a big deal with me, but it's not relevant."

Wade remained silent.

"I really loved her, you know? Like I was just going through the motions of living when I wasn't with her," Steve admitted, unable to stop himself. "From the time I was about sixteen, she was everything to me. Everything." He looked down at his clenched hands as the memories tore at him. "After her parents were killed, we were so scared that she'd be sent away somewhere. God, it was awful. Then Pauline quit college and came home. I thought our problems were over." He swallowed hard. "I was putting everything I had into football and hoping for a scholarship. For our future, you know, so I could get a degree and take care of her right."

Wade nodded. "Sounds like a good plan to me."

"Then why did it fall apart?" Steve demanded, not really expecting an answer. "We started arguing about dumb stuff. Pauline threw her a graduation party and her fiancé put the moves on Lily. Pauline saw him trying to kiss her, so she tossed her engagement ring in his face." After all this time, Steve could remember the rage he'd felt when he found out. "I wanted to beat the crap out of him, but the next thing I knew, Lily was gone. No note, no nothing. Just gone, and it no longer mattered."

"That would tend to stick in a guy's mind." Wade's voice was mild. "Have you discussed this with Lily?"

"There's no need to bring it up," Steve insisted. "I'm cool with it now." Who was he kidding? Just thinking about it made his gut churn as though it was filled with cold, greasy liquid. "I'm a lot smarter than I used to be."

"When it comes to women, men never get smarter," Wade drawled. "How's she feel about you?"

"She's all over me," Steve replied. "I'm the one in control this time." He couldn't believe he was talking about this stuff! Guys discussed sports and cars, not *relationships*.

"Oh, man," Wade exclaimed, slapping his thigh. "You might as well tie a big red bow around yourself right now, because you're a goner."

Steve shook his head. "You've got it all wrong."

"Glad to hear it." Wade looked at his watch. "I'm going to call Pauline and see if the craft project is done so I can go home. You coming?"

Steve grinned as they both stood up. "Jordan's at a sleepover. Need I say more?"

"You don't have to draw me any pictures," Wade replied as they walked back past the building. "In fact, I can do without the visuals, if you don't mind."

Much later that same evening, Lily lay cuddled up to Steve in the darkness of her bedroom. Rather than have her follow him out to his house this time, he had called a neighborhood boy to feed his dogs.

"Your place is closer," he'd pointed out with a look of pure hunger on his face. "It's got my vote."

"Mine, too, when you put it that way," she'd replied, happy that he seemed to want her more than ever. Refusing to speculate where that might take them.

"Are you hungry?" she asked him now. The night was theirs, with no one else to notice if they arrived late at the office tomorrow morning. Michelle had promised to call her cell before delivering Jordan.

"Not really," Steve replied, tightening his arm. "I'm too content to move."

"Are you sleepy?" she persisted, pleased when he shook his head. "Then why don't you tell me how you went from being a high-school senior to owning a construction company?" she suggested. "I don't even know if you went to college."

Her head was pillowed on his shoulder, her hand splayed on his chest so that she could feel his heart beating.

"I played football for the UW for a couple of years while I took classes in architecture," he began. "Spending summers building houses showed me that hands-on was what I wanted, not designing in the abstract. I went to work full-time and then I branched out on my own. That's about all there was to it."

"I'm sure it wasn't as easy as you make it sound," she murmured.

"What about you?" he asked. "When you got to Los Angeles, were you able to get any acting jobs?"

Absently, she stroked the smooth skin beneath her palm. "I tried, but the competition was beyond anything I had expected. It was expensive, too, and my share of our parents' insurance money seemed to run right through my fingers." She swallowed, recalling her panic when she realized that she was pregnant.

"I met Francis at a cattle call," she remembered aloud. "After my audition, I got sick right in the hallway and he stopped to help me. We started talking and he insisted on buying me lunch." She still felt bad that she had initially distrusted his kindness. "Before I knew it, he offered me a place to stay."

"With him?" Steve sneered.

"On his estate," she corrected. "In the guest house."

"Sounds too good to be true. What was in it for him?"

"I went places with him and we let people draw their own conclusions," she said. "I was pregnant and needed a place to stay, but I got way more than I'd hoped for. He paid for ac-counting school and he would never accept a penny for rent."

Abruptly, Steve pulled his shoulder from beneath her head and sat up. "Were you al-ready pregnant when you left Crescent Cove?"

It was the question she had hoped he would never ask. Now that he had, she realized that lying to him was out of the question. Before they could move on, he deserved the truth.

Stomach trembling with nerves, she switched the lamp on low and shifted around so she could see his face. "Yes," she admitted as she held the sheet to her breasts. "I was already pregnant. That's why I left, why I couldn't tell you. I'm sorry."

"Oh, God, sweetheart," he exclaimed in a tormented voice. "Did Carter rape you?"

Lily had never been so strongly tempted to do anything in her life as she was to allow Steve his misconception. Unless she told him otherwise, how would he ever find out? Carter had been killed in a car accident, Pauline would never betray Lily's secret and Jordan was too young to understand.

"Lily?" Steve asked when she didn't speak. "I didn't mean to remind you of something that must be painful. I'm sorry."

When he covered her hands with his, chafing away the chill that seemed to soak into her bones, she had no choice but to face a truth she had been denying for weeks.

Lord help her, but she still loved him.

All the more reason to let him go on believing that she'd had no choice in Jordan's conception. She couldn't do it, she realized with sudden clarity. If she allowed the lie to stand, someday, somehow, her son would hear that he had been the byproduct of a criminal assault.

Even to avoid hurting the man who held her future happiness in his big, work-roughened hands, she could not label her son with that terrible lie.

"No," she whispered. "Carter didn't rape me."

Dropping her hand, Steve slid out from under the covers to stand beside the bed. He folded his arms across his naked chest and stared down at Lily as though she was a bug he'd found in the sheets.

"Perhaps you'd like to explain," he suggested.

She had no choice but to get up, too, but she wasn't about to discuss something so serious without clothes. She grabbed her robe from a nearby chair and slipped it on.

His frown deepened. "Lily, were you flatbacking for one of the other guys at the same time you were holding me at arm's length? Is that when you got pregnant?" he demanded, voice as cold as her hands had been.

Lily shook her head. "I would never do that," she cried. "It was Carter. You were gone all the time and I missed you so much." Spoken aloud, her reasons sounded like such lame excuses. She forced herself to keep going. He had to understand! "Carter was an adult. He knew exactly how to play on that loneliness. I was young and starved for attention. He used that to manipulate me. I know it wasn't right, but—"

"You slept with your sister's fiancé," he finished for her. "You're right, Lily. That wasn't a very nice thing to do, but I guess the fact that you were eighteen and he was a few years older…that your boyfriend was doing everything he could to make a future for the two of you, but that you were *lonely*…why, that just makes it all hunky-dory." His voice had risen. As though he suddenly remembered that he had nothing on, he grabbed his jeans and stepped into them, not even bothering with underwear.

"Tell me," he continued as he jerked up the zipper with no regard for the tender flesh beneath it, "does Pauline agree that it was okay for you to, uh, to get it on with the man she was going to marry? Or does she even know about it?" His face was flushed, jaw clenched, as he found his shirt and yanked it on.

"She knows," Lily replied quietly, thankful that Jordan wasn't asleep down the hall. "She understands."

"I'll just bet she does." He jabbed a finger at Lily across the bed they had so recently shared. Right now, it seemed as wide as the Columbia River. "Don't kid yourself, babe. The only reason your sister is willing to have anything to do with you is because she's a sweet, loving person and you're the only family she has. You and the boy that was fathered by her very own fiancé. Talk about cozy." He braced his hands on his hips and tipped back his head.

"Man, oh, man," he exclaimed. "No wonder she broke it off with Wade while you were living under the same roof. It was *you* that she didn't trust, wasn't it?" He walked around to the end of the bed.

Lily shrank back. "It was a misunderstanding," she said through lips that felt numb. "They worked it out."

Steve's eyes glittered like chips of ice. "Did you get lonesome again? Did you try to seduce him, too?"

"I never tried to seduce Carter," she cried. "*He* came after *me*. You have no idea how much I regretted what happened. Not a day goes by—" Tears filled her eyes as she sat back down on the edge of the mattress. "I'm sorry," she gulped. "I didn't want to hurt you with the truth, so I left. I know it was wrong, wrong, wrong." She slapped the bed for emphasis. "Except for my son, I wish I could change it. He's blameless and I don't want him hurt."

Steve came around the end of the bed and leaned down so that she could feel his breath against her cheek. "But hurting me, that was okay?" He grabbed her chin and jerked it upward so she had no choice but to look straight into his eyes. "Lady, you didn't hurt me," he rasped, "you *broke* me."

He let her go and walked away, picking up the rest of his clothes as he went.

"Please try to forgive me," she begged, her pride in shreds and the pain in her heart making it almost impossible to draw a breath. "Please."

He turned in the doorway, one hand on the jamb. "Sweetheart, I should *thank* you. I tried to get over you for years. I couldn't even love my wife the way she deserved." Lifting his hand, he snapped his fingers. "And now, just like that," he said with a wide, humorless smile, "I'm over you." He made a mocking bow, complete with a sweep of his arm. "Thank you and good night."

Wordlessly Lily remained seated on the bed, listening to his heavy footsteps recede through the house, hearing the back door open and close. She pressed her hands to her ears in a futile attempt to block out the sound of his truck as he drove away. Finally, when she could no longer hear any trace of him, she threw herself across the bed and began to sob—deep, anguished cries that came straight from her own broken heart.

Chapter Twelve

Lily had no idea how long she lay on the bed after Steve left. Perhaps she dozed. The bedside lamp was still burning when her cell phone rang and she opened her swollen eyes. As though to mock her, the room was filled with sunshine.

Her mouth was dry, her throat raw. Let the damn phone ring.

Technically, it played an annoying little melody she used to like, but which she would now and forever link to this hangover she had without the party to precede it. She sat up slowly, tempted to toss her phone at the wall, but then she remembered that Michelle was supposed to call before she brought Jordan home.

Lily scrambled for her purse and dug out the offending phone before it could go to voice mail.

She'd been right; it was Michelle. "Hello," Lily croaked after clearing her throat. "How are you?"

"More important, how are *you*?" Michelle replied. "You sound awful. Are you sick?"

Sick, Lily repeated in her mind. Did feeling like her chest had been cracked and her heart hacked out count as an illness?

"I'm, uh, fine," she replied. "Just haven't had my morning coffee yet."

"Ooh, sorry, sweetie," Michelle said. "I would have called later, but Cory's got a dentist appointment and then we're going shopping in Sequim."

"No problem." The smile that Lily produced cut into her numb cheeks. "Thanks for taking him."

"Anytime," Michelle bubbled. "He's a doll and no trouble at all. I'll have him home in a little while."

After they'd ended the call, Lily bolted for the shower. There was no way she could deal with her son's inquisition if he happened to notice that she'd been crying.

Twenty minutes later when she heard a car

pull into the driveway, she was dried off and dressed. She sat at the table with her third cup of coffee and another phony smile plastered on her face like the code sticker on an apple.

"Hi, Mom!" Jordan exclaimed as he slammed the door behind him. "Cory's mom made pancakes for breakfast. He had five, but I ate six!"

Lily was relieved that Michelle hadn't decided to say hi. "I guess that makes you the pancake champ," Lily observed, gritting her teeth against the dull throb of a headache.

"Guess so." Far too mature for embarrassing displays of affection such as kissing his mom on the cheek, Jordan didn't bother coming into the kitchen. Instead he took his duffel bag down to his room.

Lily poured the rest of her coffee into the sink and set the mug into the dishwasher. Moving as though she were on automatic pilot, she swallowed a couple of ibuprofen tablets with a mouthful of tap water.

The blinking message light on her phone caught her attention. Without any real hope that Steve might have had a complete change of heart while she was in the shower, she pushed the button.

"It's Wade," said the familiar voice. "I'm

taking my job back from that bumbling im-
postor, so I'll see you in a while."

Fresh disappointment coursed through her,
followed by self-disgust that she had counted
on seeing Steve today despite the way he had
acted.

A blast of music, quickly stifled, came from
Jordan's room. She hadn't given a thought to
what she was going to tell her son when he
asked about Steve's sudden disappearance
from their lives.

With a soft moan, she rested her elbows
on the counter and laid her head against her
folded arms. Was this empty ache the same
way he had felt when he learned she was gone?
She had never wanted to think about it, but
now she had no choice but to face what she
had done.

Even if she had the words to convince him
that she was sorry, Jordan would be a con-
stant reminder of her betrayal. No one, not
even Steve, was going to make her regret the
existence of her son, she vowed silently as
she straightened.

"You look awful," Jordan said with the typ-
ical tactlessness of a twelve-year-old. "Do you
have a hangover?"

She had been too deep in thought to hear

his approach, so she'd nearly jumped a foot when he spoke. At least his question was shocking enough to take her mind off Steve for a minute.

"What did you just say to me, young man?" she demanded sternly.

"I was only trying to be funny," he whined. "Your eyes are all swollen and you're kind of white. Don't get all bent out of shape."

She could hardly believe he had noticed. Usually she got the feeling that she could have worn a red clown nose without attracting his attention, but of course he had chosen this morning to become an investigative reporter!

"I didn't sleep very well, that's all," she grumbled. "Wade's coming back to work today, so we need to get going."

"Hey, cool," Jordan replied. "Will Steve be there, too?"

She would have to get used to hearing the sound of his name without reacting. Without falling to her knees or bursting into tears.

"No." She grabbed a couple of bottles of water from the refrigerator. She hadn't packed a lunch, so they would have to buy something today. "He probably needed to get back to his own business." And his real life, the one that didn't include her.

* * *

It was another day of steady, drenching rain and gray sky, a hint of the fall weather to come. As Steve drove over to Pauline's to drop off the CDs he'd borrowed from Wade, it was hard for him to realize that the wedding was next week. Perhaps the storm clouds that seemed to have parked overhead would be replaced by sunshine by then.

He'd been at home this morning doing paperwork when the mail carrier brought him a thick envelope containing the tax receipts he'd given Lily. Even though he had checked through the entire packet, he didn't find a note from her.

As he drove past the majestic weeping willow in Pauline's front yard and turned into her driveway, he was surprised to see her SUV sitting in front of the garage. He had assumed she would be at the shop.

Since his argument with Lily, what he privately thought of as "the big reveal," he had avoided her sister, but now he couldn't very well leave again. Grabbing the CDs, he dashed through the rain and knocked on the back door.

"Hi, stranger," Pauline exclaimed with a smile. "Come on in."

"What are you doing here?" he asked after

he'd handed her the CDs. "I thought you'd be at work."

"I took the day off to get some chores done, but I need a break and I just made fresh coffee." She held the door open wider. "Come on in."

"I shouldn't stay," he said reluctantly. "Coffee sounds good, though."

"Great. I hate to drink alone."

He followed her through the laundry room into the big old-fashioned kitchen. While she busied herself at the counter, he pulled out a chair. "Is everything on schedule?"

"More or less." She must have seen his surprise, because she chuckled as she set down his mug. "I'm learning to be less regimented." She sat down across from him. "But I'm also waiting for something to go wrong, so I figure that I've got all the bases covered."

"Nothing will go wrong," he assured her. "I've never seen two people more right for each other than you and Wade."

She appeared pleased by his comment. "Coming from you, that means a lot."

She and Lily didn't look a lot alike or even share the same coloring, but this morning he could hardly look at Pauline without thinking of her sister.

"I'm glad I was home," she said, breaking the silence that had begun to grow awkward. "There's something I need to ask you."

He took a hasty sip of his coffee, nearly burning his lip. "What's that?" he asked warily.

"Is seeing Lily at the wedding going to be hard for you?" she asked bluntly. No anesthesia, not initial incision, just a stab straight to the gut.

"Why would it?" he bluffed.

She rolled her eyes. "Oh, quit being such a guy. You know exactly what I mean." She sounded exasperated.

"What has she told you?" Cautiously he risked another sip, glad the coffee was no longer scalding.

Her gaze didn't waver. "You know I'm not going to repeat it, but you can trust me, too, if you want to talk."

Her persistence began to annoy him. He didn't want to think about Lily, let alone analyze what had happened. "Just don't go there," he warned, pushing away his mug. "Leave it alone."

"Friends don't let friends warn them off," Pauline teased gently. "Who else do you have to talk to besides Wade? And you know he'll just tell you what you want to hear."

Steve doubted that very much as he tried to stare her down. Obviously, she was prepared to wait him out as she folded her arms and leaned back in her chair.

"How can you pretend that the past never happened?" he demanded. "Your own sister *humiliated* you. Hell, until Wade came along, you always worried what people thought about you. It was like you didn't measure up because you'd made one bad choice in your life."

It was Pauline's turn to look startled. "It was Carter who humiliated me, not Lily," she crisply. "Maybe Wade was the catalyst, but at least I got past it."

Was she implying that he hadn't? "Look, I'm sorry," he said, shifting uncomfortably. "We both know that we're not just talking about some kiss at her party. How can you dismiss what happened as though it didn't matter? For God's sake, she had his *child.*"

"I'd be lying if I told you it didn't hurt terribly," Pauline admitted. "I thought we were past it and then she told me about Jordan." She glanced out the window, swallowing hard. "I felt as though I'd been dragged right back into that dark hole, but then I realized that Lily was a victim, too."

All Steve could do was to gape in silent

disbelief. Had the stress of planning her wedding done something to her mind?

"Have you ever considered what she went through?" Pauline asked. "Until Francis Yost literally took her in, she was all alone in a strange city, dealing with an unplanned pregnancy and the challenge of being a single mother. She must have been terrified."

Steve didn't want to think of Lily as a damned victim! What he wanted was to clap his hands over his ears to prevent Pauline's words from striking at his sense of conviction.

Unfortunately for him, she wasn't finished. "I forgave my sister because I saw what I wanted in Carter, so clearly I, too, make mistakes. Someday, I might need a little of that forgiveness, too."

"You were young and Carter Black was a sleaze," Steve began.

She reached across the table to pat his hand. "Exactly."

He shook his head. "I didn't mean—"

"We all need second chances." She drew back with a slight chuckle. "Now I sound like the mom from *Happy Days*, but I hate to see the two of you so unhappy. I thought you'd found your way back to each other."

He jerked back as though she'd taken a swing

at him. "Let me get one thing straight," he insisted. "I was plenty angry when I found out about Carter, but that was because of before. This time around, Lily and I weren't serious."

Pauline appeared puzzled. "If what happened with Carter is tied to the past, why does it bother you so much now?"

Her logic yawned before him like a pit full of sharpened stakes. It was a trap.

"This is pointless!" he huffed. "Lily and I are both adults. I'm not brokenhearted and neither is she."

Pauline leaned forward and clasped her hands together on the table, her engagement ring sparkling in the light. It reminded him of Wade's excitement when he'd showed up at Steve's job site to announce his engagement.

"When she left, did you ever try to get her back?" Pauline asked, changing direction abruptly.

His temper flared. "Did you?"

She looked down at the table. "No, I didn't. She loved us both and we let her down."

He'd had enough. He didn't want to hear how he had let Lily down, because then he would start to wonder whether his anger was justified or he was just letting her down again.

He shoved back his chair. "Thanks for the

coffee," he said as he got to his feet. "I've got to get going."

Pauline followed him to the back door. "Take care," she said, touching his shoulder. "I just want you to be happy."

Steve nodded. "I know. I'll see you later."

As he climbed into his truck, he tried without success to block thoughts of Lily. If everyone deserved a second chance, why was he holding her accountable for mistakes she had made in the past?

He slapped his hand against the wheel hard enough to sting. For once, he had no answer.

Lily was thankful that she'd been so busy opening her business, getting Jordan ready for school and helping Pauline with last-minute wedding details. If Lily had possessed a spare moment to think about Steve and how much she missed him, she didn't think she could have managed it.

After being so instrumental in helping with the office remodel, he had missed the open house because he was in Arizona visiting his parents. Even without his presence, the event had gone well.

A decent crowd had shown up for the free appetizers and cake, the local press had sent a photographer and Gail Harris, the new office manager, had managed the details with unobtrusive efficiency. Both Lily and Wade had been kept busy seeing prospective clients ever since.

She and Michelle had taken the boys school-shopping at the Silverdale Mall, then Lily had enrolled Jordan for sixth grade at the local elementary school, which was only a few blocks away. On the first day of class, he insisted on going without her. Filled with anxiety, Lily hadn't been able to concentrate on a thing until he came home again.

Although her questions had been met with mostly one-word replies, he hadn't seemed the least bit traumatized by the experience. A huge load of guilt for dragging him to Crescent Cove lifted from her shoulders as she breathed a sigh of relief. He had even stopped asking when he was going to see Steve again.

With her new business attracting clients, her son safely enrolled in school and her sister's wedding on track, Lily figured that only a totally self-centered and selfish individual would want more. She tried desperately to convince herself that she was—if not ecstatically happy with her life—at least reasonably content.

By sheer determination, she was slowly learning to cut off thoughts of Steve as soon as they intruded. When Pauline dragged her along to the next meeting of the Crescent Cove Business Owners' Association and a reasonably attractive attorney asked her to dinner, she forced herself to accept.

"Good for you," Pauline said on the ride home. "I'm glad you're moving on."

Lily's reply had been to burst into tears. "When does the hurting stop?" she'd asked, embarrassed by her lapse.

"I guess it depends on how long it takes to get over someone," Pauline replied, patting Lily's hand.

"Isn't thirteen years long enough?" Lily murmured with a sigh, not really expecting an answer.

"Have you tried talking to Steve?" Pauline asked as she stopped for a red light. "He's not an unreasonable person."

"I've thought of calling, but what would I say?" Lily replied, twisting the soggy tissue in her fingers. "I did what I did and nothing will change that."

"That's true." The light turned green and they went on through the intersection. "If you can't change something, you have to change how you deal with it. I'm not saying this to make you feel bad," she continued briskly, "but after you left, he had to endure all the gossip, too, the same as I did. Even if he's still crazy about you, the idea of being humiliated again might be more than he can overcome."

Not to mention his belief that he might not be able to father a child, Lily realized. Suddenly she straightened in her seat. "That's it!" she exclaimed with a rush of excitement. "I need to figure out a way to show him that it won't happen again. That I won't embarrass him in front of the entire town."

"Hmm, maybe you're on to something." Pauline didn't sound too convinced as she pulled into her driveway next to Lily's car and braked her SUV. "How are you going to accomplish all that?"

Lily slumped back against the seat. "I haven't the faintest idea."

She followed her sister into the house to thank Wade for keeping an eye on Jordan. Her son had insisted that he was old enough now to stay alone. Perhaps he was right, especially with an aunt and almost-uncle a phone call away. So far, Jordan had come home from school every day without incident. Basically, he was a reliable, levelheaded kid, so he would probably be fine in the evenings, as well. *She* was the one who got nervous about it, not him.

After they got home, he played a game on his computer while she sat in front of the television. The reality show that was on failed to hold her interest; instead she kept trying to come up with a plan to convince Steve that they deserved another chance. And that she wasn't going to leave him again, not ever.

The next morning on her way back to town from meeting a client who wanted Lily to handle the quarterly state tax return for her business, she drove past a reader-board that was prominently displayed in front of a small print shop.

Bob is 65! Happy Birthday.

How clever, she thought, and how publicly embarrassing. Her car swerved abruptly as realization dawned. This might be an answer to her prayers. With a glance in her mirror, she turned into the parking lot. Less than ten minutes later, she came back out to her car. For the first time in weeks, she was filled with encouragement.

By the time she got to the office, she was humming along with the radio.

"Don't you look pleased with yourself,"

Gail remarked when Lily walked through the front door.

The reception area had turned out just as she'd envisioned it. The wood floor had been refinished in satiny cherry. Leather chairs, glass tables and elegant brass lamps formed an inviting seating area. In the former dining room was the reception area, Gail's workspace.

"I just signed up a new client," Lily replied. She handed the other woman a folder containing Claudia Mallard's information. "I'll be in my office."

My office, my office, my office, she chanted silently as she went down the freshly painted hallway. Saying the words still gave her a feeling of satisfaction.

Seated behind her new desk, she called the attractive attorney to cancel their dinner date.

"I'm sorry," she said when he picked up the phone. "I suppose I could make excuses, but the truth is that I should never have accepted your invitation. It's not you, believe me. I've got feelings for someone else."

"I won't tell you that I'm not disappointed." He had a deep voice, an asset for a trial lawyer. "Or curious," he added, "but I'm due in court, so I'll just wish you luck. If things don't work out, give me a call."

Relieved, she replaced the receiver when her cell phone sounded from the depths of her purse. With a flutter of fresh concern, she dug it out. As soon as she saw that the call was from an LA area code, curiosity replaced alarm.

"Lily, I've got great news," announced the attorney handling Francis's estate. "We've got a solid offer on the property from a pre-approved buyer."

Chapter Thirteen

Steve had a pretty good idea that the reason he'd been invited to Pauline and Wade's for dinner just a few days before the wedding was because they were worried about him. He didn't care; Pauline's home-cooked pot roast with vegetables and gravy was worth a little misplaced pity.

All through the meal, which she served at the huge antique dining room table beneath a fancy crystal chandelier, the conversation ambled from the Mariners to the Seahawks, the fate of the Alaskan Way Viaduct, which had been damaged by the last earthquake, to whether a third floating bridge would ever be built across Lake Washington.

They asked about the house he was finally going to start. Pauline filled him in on her plans to expand her shop into the recently vacated space next door and Wade bragged a little about how well his new business was going.

"You'll never guess who came to see me," Wade said over bowls of marionberry sherbet. "Pauline's nemesis, Harriet Tuttle and her husband, Elroy."

"Oh?" Steve was surprised. "I always figured they must have a little something tucked away for a rainy day."

Harriet was descended from one of the founding families of Crescent Cove. An ancestor had owned a lumber mill back in the late 1800s when the town was a booming commercial hub. She had also led the charge against Pauline when she had dared to rent a room in her house to Wade, even though at the time there had been nothing illicit between them.

Wade winked as he spooned up more sherbet. "Their information is confidential, of course, but let's just say they could buy a lot of umbrellas if they wanted."

"Good for you," Steve replied, finishing his

dessert. "Pauline, sweetie, the meal was wonderful. Now I've got a little news of my own." He took a swallow of water for his suddenly dry mouth and then he cleared his throat nervously.

"I thought about what you said," he told her, "that everyone needs second chances and that Lily was a victim, too."

It was Pauline's turn to say "Oh?" as she exchanged a quick glance with Wade.

Steve figured the two of them had discussed what a pigheaded fool he'd been. Maybe they were right, maybe not. Either way, he was ready to give Lily a chance to explain.

Hell, he might as well go whole hog and admit the truth. "I love her," he said bluntly. "Yeah, I love her." The words felt good on his tongue. They felt right. "I blamed my divorce on a lot of different things, but the truth is that I wasn't fair to Christie. I couldn't be, because I hadn't gotten over Lily. I'm headed over there right now so I can tell her how I feel."

Pauline's eyes filled with tears, making his stomach lurch and then plunge right down to his toes.

"What's wrong?" he demanded, gaze shifting between her and Wade. "Is Lily okay? Has something happened?"

Again Pauline exchanged a glance with Wade before she spoke. "I guess you haven't heard. Lily and Jordan left this afternoon. They've gone back to LA."

Steve heard the words, but it took him a moment to absorb the meaning behind them. She had left again! He could scarcely believe it.

He slid back his chair, his hands fisted and his jaw clenched with determination as he rose. "She can't do this to me again. I won't let her. This time I'm going after her. I'll bring them back where they belong, even if I have to drag her by her pretty blond hair."

To his surprise, Wade, too, got to his feet. Wearing a big grin, he clapped a hand on Steve's rigid shoulder. "Relax, pal. I'm glad to hear you've come to your senses and all that, but they aren't gone for good. Lily had to sign some papers down there, that's all. They'll be home in a day or two."

Torn between feeling foolish and relieved, Steve slumped back into his chair. "You know what, I don't think I'm going to wait around for her this time."

Pauline looked alarmed. "They'll be back for the wedding. Lily promised."

"I'm going after them," he insisted. "You must know where they're staying."

Lily got out of the rental car and walked to the gate across the long, curved driveway of the sprawling estate where she had lived for the past thirteen years of her life. Tomorrow, she would officially sign the paper accepting the offer that Max had described on the phone. Half of the proceeds would go to Francis's partner, the rest into a trust fund for Jordan. Lily's former mentor had already left her a generous amount of money, but he had wanted to provide for her son's college tuition, as well.

Perhaps it was foolish of her to come here tonight, since she had known that the elaborate wrought-iron gate would be locked and Max had the keys. She had dropped Jordan at his best buddy's house. She hadn't wanted to upset him by bringing him here, but his friend's mother had told Lily to take as long as she liked.

She stared up at the empty windows in the main house, a traditional stucco structure with a red-tiled roof. In the moonlight, she could see that the landscape service had done a good job maintaining the grounds and the flowers Francis had loved.

"What would I have done without you?" she murmured aloud, hands wrapped around two of the iron bars as she peered through the gate. "I hope you know how much I appreciate everything you did for me and my son." Tears filled her eyes and blurred her vision as a car passed on the main road that wound through the luxurious neighborhood.

"You were right about Steve," she continued as though it were perfectly normal to be talking to a dead man. People did it all the time in cemeteries, so why not here where she felt his presence so strongly? "He's great with Jordan and it doesn't matter to me that we might not have more kids. This time I'm not letting him go."

She aimed a tremulous smile at the upstairs window. Every time she had arrived home through these gates, she would look up and wave in case he was looking. Now she spent several more minutes describing the business she had launched, Jordan's school and the house they were leasing.

"I guess it's time to say goodbye," she said. "I'm not totally happy yet, but I'm working on it. Thanks for giving me the chance." Her voice dropped to a whisper. "I love you."

She waved at the empty window for the last

time and then she dabbed at her cheeks with her fingers. As she was about to get back into the car, a taxi pulled up behind it. Shielding her eyes with her hand, Lily squinted at the headlights. A prickle of nervousness slithered up her spine as the back door opened and a male figure emerged, silhouetted against the bright glow.

"Lily, you aren't easy to find," he said.

Recognition jolted through her. "What are you doing here?" she cried. "How did you know where I was?"

Steve ducked down to speak to the cab driver. When he slammed the door, the taxi backed onto the street again and drove away. Hands in his pockets, he approached her slowly as her eyes adjusted to the relative darkness.

"Pauline gave me this address, as well as the hotel where you were staying," he said as easily as if they'd happened on each other at the local Safeway back in Crescent Cove. "I went there first, as soon as my flight landed, and then I decided to play a hunch." He stopped a few feet away, but she could see his face clearly now in the moonlight.

"When she first said you'd come back to LA, I couldn't breathe," he added. "I thought you'd left again. Do you know why I'm here, Lily Marlene?"

He hadn't used her middle name like that since high school when it had always meant he was about to tell her something very serious.

She took a step forward on shaky legs. "I hope you're here because you've decided to give me another chance," she said softly, her lower lip trembling. Why else would he have followed her all the way out here?

When he shook his head slowly, indicating that she was wrong, the lump that had formed in her throat threatened to choke her. Had she completely misread the situation? Had something happened to Pauline or Wade?

Before she could voice her alarm, he closed the gap between them and extended his hand. Trying hard not to start crying again as hope rose like a bright balloon, she clutched his fingers, savoring the warmth of his skin and the strength of his grip. She had missed him so much!

"I've been a real jackass," he said gruffly. "Can you ever forgive me?"

Forgive *him?* Didn't he have that backward?

"I don't understand," she replied. "I'm the

one who was wrong. I've made so many mistakes."

"Jordan's not a mistake, and neither is the job you've done to raise him, or the choices you made to give him a better life." He took a deep breath and she realized that he, too, was nervous.

"I can't tell you how much I've grown to respect you since you came home," he said, voice growing husky. "When we were kids, I loved your beauty, your laugh, the way you made me feel when you cuddled up next to me like I was your hero. But now that we're adults, I realize there's so much more to you than appearance."

She was unable to prevent the tears from welling up. When she tried to blink them away, they spilled over and ran down her face. "I don't know what to say," she whispered, deeply touched.

Gently, he touched his finger to her cheek, catching one of her tears. "Yes, you do," he urged.

As she studied his face, absorbing everything, her heart began to melt and she was flooded with unbelievable happiness. It was time for her to lay it on the line, to take the leap without the net.

"I love you," she said simply. "You're truly the only one for me."

For a moment, he squeezed his eyes shut and then he pulled her into his arms. "Ah, Lily," he murmured against her hair, "I never got over you. I love you, too."

When she lifted her head, the kiss he gave her started out as a sweet confirmation of their feelings. Then, as she crowded as close to him as she could get, he groaned deep in his throat. His arms tightened, molding her even tighter to his straining male body. The kiss changed as they each struggled to show the other how desperately they had been missed.

When a noisy sports car sped by and Lily came up for air, she was startled to find herself up against the side of her rental car. Then Steve stunned her even more by dropping down on one knee in the driveway.

"I should have come after you years ago," he said, capturing both her hands in his. "I may be a slow learner, but I'm not a total idiot."

He paused as her heart hammered in her chest. "Marry me, Lily. If I can't give you children, we'll figure out something else, I swear. I'll do everything I can to make you happy, but there's never been anyone else for me and there never will. I'm totally at your mercy."

At some point, her tears had stopped without her noticing. Now she gave him a smile of pure joy.

"Of course I'll marry you," she exclaimed. "Your love is everything I need to complete my life. The rest doesn't matter."

His answering smile brimmed with love. "I'll buy you a ring as soon as we get home," he promised. "Since Pauline has gotten to be such an expert when it comes to planning weddings, maybe she'll help you with ours so we won't have to wait too long."

Lily tugged one of her hands free and reached up to rest her palm against his cheek. "The sooner, the better," she agreed, happier than she'd ever been. "I just want to be your wife."

He got to his feet and brushed off his knee. "I don't have a hotel reservation. Can I stay with you so we can all fly home together?"

Lily couldn't help but chuckle at his pleading expression. "Sure thing, but you know I'm the mother of an impressionable sixth-grader. You'll have to share a room with him."

To his credit, Steve's smile didn't slip. "If you say so."

As he opened the car door for her, she glanced one last time at that empty window in Francis's house. For an instant, she thought she saw something there. Before she could be sure, it was gone again. Probably just a reflection, she told herself silently.

As she rode back to the hotel with Steve, she suddenly remembered the reader board message she'd ordered on the way into Crescent Cove.

"I've got a surprise for you when we get home," she told Steve, who was still holding her hand.

"What is it?" he wheedled. "Come on, tell me."

Lily shook her head firmly. "No way. You'll have to wait until we get back. Trust me, though. You'll know it when you see it."

With a private little grin, she pictured the sign in her head:

Lily loves Steve
Always has, always will

* * * * *

HOMETOWN HEARTS ♥

YES! Please send me **The Hometown Hearts Collection** in Larger Print. This collection begins with 3 FREE books and 2 FREE gifts in the first shipment. Along with my 3 free books, I'll also get the next 4 books from the Hometown Hearts Collection, in LARGER PRINT, which I may either return and owe nothing, or keep for the low price of $4.99 U.S./ $5.89 CDN each plus $2.99 for shipping and handling per shipment*. If I decide to continue, about once a month for 8 months I will get 6 or 7 more books, but will only need to pay for 4. That means 2 or 3 books in every shipment will be FREE! If I decide to keep the entire collection, I'll have paid for only 32 books because 19 books are FREE! I understand that accepting the 3 free books and gifts places me under no obligation to buy anything. I can always return a shipment and cancel at any time. My free books and gifts are mine to keep no matter what I decide.

262 HCN 3432 462 HCN 3432

Name _____ (PLEASE PRINT) _____

Address _____ Apt. # _____

City _____ State/Prov. _____ Zip/Postal Code _____

Signature (if under 18, a parent or guardian must sign)

Mail to the **Reader Service:**
IN U.S.A.: P.O. Box 1867, Buffalo, NY. 14240-1867
IN CANADA: P.O. Box 609, Fort Erie, Ontario L2A 5X3

* Terms and prices subject to change without notice. Prices do not include applicable taxes. Sales tax applicable in NY. Canadian residents will be charged applicable taxes. This offer is limited to one order per household. All orders subject to approval. Credit or debit balances in a customer's account(s) may be offset by any other outstanding balance owed by or to the customer. Please allow 4 to 6 weeks for delivery. Offer available while quantities last. Offer not available to Quebec residents.

Your Privacy—The Reader Service is committed to protecting your privacy. Our Privacy Policy is available online at www.ReaderService.com or upon request from the Reader Service.

We make a portion of our mailing list available to reputable third parties that offer products we believe may interest you. If you prefer that we not exchange your name with third parties, or if you wish to clarify or modify your communication preferences, please visit us at www.ReaderService.com/consumerschoice or write to us at Reader Service Preference Service, P.O. Box 9062, Buffalo, NY. 14240-9062. Include your complete name and address.

Get 2 Free Books,
Plus 2 Free Gifts—
just for trying the Reader Service!

Get 2 Free Books,
Plus 2 Free Gifts—
just for trying the
Reader Service!

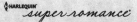

Get 2 Free Books,
Plus 2 Free Gifts—
just for trying the Reader Service!

HARLEQUIN

HEARTWARMING™